of the
MOUNTAIN

THE KINGS
OF THE
MOUNTAIN

Clare Cooper

Pont Books

First published by Hodder and Stoughton 1986
New edition by Pont Books, Gomer Press 1994

ISBN 1 85902 080 1

Published with the support of the Welsh Arts Council.

Printed by J. D. Lewis & Sons Ltd.,
Gomer Press, Llandysul, Dyfed

Preface

When Simon Jones came to live on the mountain in West Wales he had no idea that he was a wizard. Then he met a girl called Fred who showed him the wonderful Black Horn hanging on the wall of her Aunt Meryl's house, and not only did Simon then discover that he could make magic with the Black Horn, but he also found that he had Second Sight and a great, magic power in his hands as well.

Simon and Fred rescued a Unicorn which had been trapped on the mountain, and Fred was then convinced that Simon was the legendary Second Wizard of the Black Horn. Later, Simon met a witch called Blodwen Emmanuel who agreed with Fred and told him that one day he would be a very great wizard indeed.

Now, gradually, Simon is beginning to enjoy making magic, and as the months pass by he is discovering many more interesting things about himself and the magic he can make. Fred is a great help to him, but she does tend to rush him into doing things before he is ready to do them, and some of the things he can do with the Black Horn still worry him, too.

However, his mountain (especially the carn on the summit), and the mysterious, magic Islands in the mist, where he left the Unicorn, always give him joy and keep him determined to be very good at magic—but terrible things do happen, and he does come across some very unpleasant people who are also very good at magic.

1. Dewi Llewelyn

Simon sat on his bedroom window-sill and looked up across the green, brown and purple mountain to the dark, grey blur which he knew was the carn. He closed his eyes and imagined it, remembering it so much more clearly than he could see it with his poor eyes and thick-lensed spectacles. The stones of the carn were rough and lichen-covered, with specks of bright metal catching the gold of the sun. The lichen was golden too, well, yellow really, bright yellow, with greyish frills which blended with the stones. The hoverflies which seemed to haunt the place were yellow and black. He hadn't seen any hoverflies for a while.

He wondered if he would be able to see the hoverflies if he sat there with the Black Horn in his hands. It was an interesting thought. He opened his eyes, blinking owlishly at the light. 'I've never tried to do that,' he thought. 'I ought to try. It would be a sort of experiment. Experimenting's a good way to find out things—but what is it I'm trying to find out exactly?' He thought carefully about this for a while and decided that the question he was trying to answer with this experiment was: 'Is it only magic things that I can see clearly with the Black Horn in my hands, or can I see ordinary things clearly then too?'

The Black Horn stood in its place beside his bed. He reached out and picked it up, and turned back to the window. Now he could see every detail of the stones of the magic carn, but he still couldn't see the hoverflies. So, it was only an actual magic place that he could see with the help of the horn. 'And anything to to with magic that happens to be on it,' he thought, as he remembered seeing the Unicorn high on the carn last summer. 'And is there anything magic on it today?' he wondered.

Half hopefully, half ruefully, smiling to himself at his own whimsy, he looked again. His smile faded. He *could* see something on the carn. He could see something moving. Was its some*thing*, or some*one*? He stood there, hardly daring to breathe as the moving shape seemed to crystallise and take substance as it reached the level, grass patch near the summit. It was a person, a person on horseback, and, what was more, it was a person he knew. It was Dewi Llewelyn.

Simon put down the horn quickly. Dewi Llewelyn of all people! He didn't like seeing Dewi Llewelyn anywhere, and he certainly didn't want to be able to see him on the carn. He blinked up at it. Now he couldn't see him. That felt better. But that was silly.

He was being stupid. Dewi was still there. He ought to look at him.

Reluctantly, he picked up the Black Horn again, and stood, holding it, as he stared up at the rider etched clearly against the grey sky. 'Dewi Llewelyn!' He would know that face anywhere. 'Beastly, bigheaded Dewi!' Simon made himself watch the

face he disliked so much, and found, as he watched it with the Horn in his hands, that, even though he didn't like that face, he had to admit that it was a very interesting one. He began to wonder about Dewi.

'He looks *right* up there,' he thought. 'He fits in, sitting there on that horse with all that untidy hair blowing in the wind. He looks like an Apache. No! He looks like a—like a son of an ancient warrior. Yes! That's what he looks like, a prince from the old days, with a nose like an eagle's beak and black eyebrows that make his face look cruel. But he's not cruel, not really. He's just bigheaded. And if only he wouldn't make fun of me and call me "idiot"!'

Simon thought bitterly of what seemed like the hundreds of times at school when Dewi had told jokes about him and made the whole class fall about laughing. 'Jokes!' he thought. 'What's funny about me being good at maths? And what's funny about me coming here from Petts Wood? He knows he's not really being funny. He's just being mickey-taking and beastly!' He looked at Dewi closely again. 'He looks different up there. And what's he *doing* up there . . . ?'

As soon as he had asked himself the question, Simon knew the answer, and he didn't like that, either. Dewi quite obviously, was sitting up there on his horse, on the carn, gazing out across the sea at the Islands, the beautiful, mysterious Islands in the mist, the Islands which could only be seen by people with Second Sight. Simon could see them. He had Second Sight. And so, quite obviously, had Dewi Llewelyn.

Simon felt quite cold as he realised it. Dewi Llewelyn with Second Sight. Dewi Llewelyn a special person like himself. It was an awful thought, but, somehow, not altogether surprising, for, as Simon watched Dewi turn his horse and disappear behind the carn, he realised that he had known for quite a long time that Dewi was complicated with magic. 'Ever since I realised about the dark side of the mountain,' he thought.

Dewi lived on the other side of the mountain, the side which Simon had always thought of as the 'dark' side. Several months ago if he had been asked why he called it the 'dark' side, he would have said that it was because it was the side which was hidden from the sunlit Islands. But during the last few months he had found out something new about the magic in himself. He had discovered that, not only was there magic in his hands, but there was also a part of his mind which told him when other people, or places, were complicated with magic.

He had discovered it when he had been visiting his friend, Blodwen Emmanuel, the old woman who knew everything. Usually when he visited her in the dark narrow valley where she lived, he found her at home in her kitchen, but, one day, he had met her walking to meet him . . . and he had known that she was there long before he saw her. Some part of his mind had told him that she was there.

And, on another day, soon after that, when he was looking at the bleak stretch of moorland where Dewi lived, he had realised that he called it 'dark' because this special part of his mind was telling him that was what it was . . . a place complicated by the powers of darkness.

'And Dewi lives there,' he thought. 'Yes, of course, I've always known that he was different, just like I'm different. I just didn't want to admit it, that's all.' He began to worry.

He thought at first that it was a coincidence when his mother began talking about the Llewelyn family that evening, but, when he thought about it again, he realised that it probably wasn't a coincidence at all, for the reason which made his mother talk about them was probably the same reason which had sent Dewi to the carn to look at the Islands. 'He feels better about things when he looks at the Islands, just like I do,' Simon thought, as he listened to his mother telling him that Dewi's grandmother was dying.

'She's all but a hundred!' Mother said. 'Ninety-nine—what an age! And now she's going to just miss her telegram from the Queen, or whatever they get these days.' She went on to talk about Dewi's father. 'He's called Amahiah, you know. Amahiah!'

'I like it,' Dad said. 'He must be Chapel. Do I know him, Dil?'

'You must know him by sight. He's that thin little man who looks like he must be the original for a Kyffin Williams painting of a hill farmer.'

'Rides in to the town on a brown cob with a sack for a saddle?'

'That's the one.'

Simon knew who they meant. Amahiah Llewelyn was a sour-looking man. 'He's got a face like Dewi's too,' he thought, 'all beak and eyebrows. And I bet he's just as beastly. But *was* Dewi up there on the carn to cheer himself up with a look at the Islands?' The thought unsettled Simon. It didn't fit at all with the idea he had of the sort of person Dewi was. He needed to think about Dewi.

He went back upstairs to sit quietly on his own. The carn was a black, looming shadow now, just a shape against the stormy sky. He watched the sky. Heavy clouds swept across, low behind the carn, racing each other, intent on shutting out the crescent moon, but, again and again, the moon broke through the black barrier the clouds had thrown between it and the carn, again and again, it came racing, hurrying, speeding through the night.

Simon watched the moon. It was fascinating. How quickly it seemed to go! It seemed to be racing, all alone up there, across some wide, twilight country which was hidden from him by clouds as heavy and dark as rock. It was strange the way it looked, odd. He could watch it all night. But the clouds banked up and fell and spread across the sky, and now he couldn't even see the carn. The moon was gone. The carn was gone. But there was something there.

Simon peered at the mountain, at a cluster of small, winking lights, and an odd idea came into his head that these lights were stars, stars on the mountain, fallen stars. He stood rigid, afraid to move. Were they stars, stars on the mountain?

The group of lights twinkled and moved just below the carn. 'They're on the path,' he thought. 'They're not stars. They're torches. No, not torches . . . lanterns! There are people up there carrying lanterns.'

The lights spread out and became a line of flickering specks of white which wound, slowly and steadily, down the mountain path. As he watched it, something about the quality of the lights, some frailty, some eeriness, made Simon reach for the Black Horn. These were no ordinary lights. These lights he must look at properly.

With the Horn in his hands, he could see at once exactly what the lights were. He watched them, fascinated and frightened. The lights were 'canhwyllau corff,' ghostly funeral candles, carried by weird, phantom figures as they bore a phantom coffin towards its grave. He had read about this. This sort of thing had happened many times before. This was a vision which foretold a funeral, a vision which came with death. Someone on the mountain had just died.

Simon knew who it must be. It must be old Mrs Llewelyn, ninety-nine and just missed her telegram from the Queen. But that wasn't what he thought about as he watched the sad and terrible procession, He thought: 'Canhwyllau corff . . . corpse candles . . . magic . . . and it's for Dewi's grandmother.'

Dewi's grandmother, he decided, must have been as complicated with magic as he was himself, but *her* magic, and Dewi's too, was the magic of darkness, the magic which he could feel on the dark side of the mountain.

2. A Talk on a Bus

Simon's mother heard in the village next day that old Mrs Llewelyn had died. 'She's to be buried the day after tomorrow,' she told them. 'They say the boy, the grandson, is going to sing at the funeral.' She turned to Simon eagerly. 'Do you know him at school?' she asked. 'Has he got a lovely voice?'

'Well, yes,' Simon said, 'I suppose so. He does sing a lot, but then, everybody does.' The way the children at this Welsh school were able and even eager to get up and sing or recite the moment they were asked, amazed Simon. The very thought of singing in public made him hot and confused and completely dry of throat. He lived in dread that some day he might be asked to do it. But they were not at all embarrassed. He sometimes thought they must have learned to sing and say poetry before they could talk, it came so naturally to them.

He thought of Dewi singing. 'I suppose he can sing

better than most of them,' he admitted. 'It's him they always get to sing at concerts and that sort of thing.'

'What does he sing?' Simon's mother was thoroughly interested. 'Hymns?' She was thinking of Mr Llewelyn being called Amahiah, Simon supposed.

'No,' he said, 'not hymns. Actually, he always sings in Welsh, so I don't know exactly what they are, not all of them. Most of them are folk songs, but he likes to slip in a sort of rebel one if he can, now and then, especially to annoy the headmaster, I think.'

'Good heavens!' His mother looked alarmed. But Simon grinned. It always pleased him to see Dewi annoying the headmaster. When he saw the headmaster suffering in outraged silence, he always thought: 'I'm in good company.'

Dewi didn't come back to school until after the day of the funeral, and when he came back everyone could see at once that something had happened to him. He wouldn't talk to anyone. He sat, alone, quietly, almost nervously. He wouldn't join in lessons or games, and, worst of all, he wouldn't sing. They asked him to, but he wouldn't. He shook his head and said: 'I can't,' and then he turned his back on them all and stared out of the window, so they left him alone.

Simon noticed that he was still alone at break. At lunch time he found him in the far corner of the rugby field, where Simon had been told that he would have been able to see the carn, if he had had ordinary good eyes. During the afternoon break he looked to see if he was there again, but he couldn't see him there, or anywhere else, until he realised, with an unpleasant shock, that Dewi was standing close to him, watching him. He walked away, but when he looked around again, Dewi was still there, uncomfortably close, still watching. And then, on the bus on the way home, Dewi came and sat beside him.

Simon expected the worst . . . teasing all the way home, or else a tirade of loud complaints because he, Simon, lived on Dewi's mountain. That was what usually happened at moments like this.

But Dewi sat in silence. For at least three miles he said absolutely nothing. He didn't even look at Simon. Then, when the first glimpse of the carn appeared across the hedges and the fields, he sighed. 'Jones,' he said quietly. 'I want you to meet me up there tonight.'

Simon didn't even try to keep the suspicion out of his voice. 'Why?' he asked.

For the first time that day Dewi grinned. 'The little lad fears the worst,' he said to no one in particular. Then he looked at Simon. 'Have no fear, I don't mean to lure you to the mugging of your life, Jones bach. That's not my style, is it? And I won't even take the Michael . . . much; No, I just want to talk to you, see.'

'What about?'

'Ah, still I detect suspicion in his voice. If I could tell you what about and why, I'd talk to you here, idiot,' Dewi said. 'No, I'll tell you up there, tonight. I'll give you an hour to have your tea, then see you.'

Simon longed to say 'No', to refuse absolutely to go anywhere with Dewi, and especially not to go anywhere near the carn. But he couldn't say 'No'. He knew he mustn't. This was a request, not to him, Simon Jones, but to Jones the Wizard of the Black Horn, and he was duty-bound to say 'Yes'. Though, quite honestly, even if it had been only Dewi asking him, Simon, to meet him, he would probably still have said 'Yes'. He was a little too afraid of Dewi to risk arguing.

He climbed down from the bus, feeling absolutely miserable. Dewi Llewelyn, on the carn, alone. 'And what does he want anyway?' Despair set in, hard. And then, there was Fred waiting for him in the lane, with Gwenhwyfar the white donkey, and Bedwyr the ancient terrier. And Fred shouldn't have been there at all.

'What are you doing here?' Simon began to smile

again. 'You can't have broken up. It isn't even half-term.'

'It is for us.' Fred went to a boarding school. 'We have a fortnight this half-term. It's so that all the new little darlings who aren't used to being away from Mummy have something decent to look forward to when they're left all on their own after the summer.'

'What a good idea!'

'Great, isn't it! But to look at you, Jonesy, I'd say *you* look as though you need something to look forward to, too. Your face was as long as a fiddle when you got off the bus. Had a day of it in school, have you?'

'You could say that.'

Simon told Fred about Dewi as they walked together along the lane towards his home, Tŷ Corn Du Bach. He told her about the dark side of the mountain, too, and about the corpse candles for old Mrs Llewelyn.

'Brass bedknobs, how gruesome!' Fred was thrilled and horrified, he could see. 'What did they look like, the phantoms? Could you see them?'

'They were beastly—horrible.' Simon began to feel despair settling on him again.

'She was pretty beastly and horrible herself, by all accounts,' Fred said.

20

'Was she?' Simon was interested but not surprised.

'Oh, I've heard people talking about her—Meryl for one, and Daniel—brass bedknobs! Daniel!' Fred stood still and stared at Simon.

She looked excited, and Simon waited rather apprehensively to hear who Daniel was and why he should be significant. Fred's sudden excitement when he was telling her about some problem of his, usually meant trouble, or, at least, no peace until he had done something about what ever it was that she felt significant enough to be exciting. 'Who's Daniel?' he asked.

'Daniel Llewelyn! He's Dewi's uncle, or something. He's related, anyhow. Brass bedknobs, what a coincidence this is.'

'What's a coincidence?' Simon was now *very* apprehensive.

'That you should be having trouble with Dewi just when Daniel has turned up at Tŷ Corn Du again.'

Tŷ Corn Du was Fred's home. She explained to Simon as they walked along again, that Daniel Llewelyn was an old man who had once been a gardener at Tŷ Corn Du. 'It was when Grandfather was alive and we could still afford a gardener. We had a housekeeper too, but that's beside the point.'

'What *is* the point?'

'That Daniel Llewelyn should be working for us again just when you're having something to do with his nephew.' Fred chattered on. She quite obviously liked Daniel. 'I say *working,* but really all he's doing is giving advice. He's much too old to work at gardening. You know, all the heavy stuff. But he knows exactly how the garden used to look, so Guy's got him to tell the blokes who're actually doing the job exactly what to do and how to do it.' She laughed. 'He's terribly fussy. He's got some great Welsh swear words which I wish somebody would translate. And do you know what, Jonesy, he's going to give me a ferret.'

'A ferret! Gosh, aren't they dangerous?'

'No, not a bit—as long as they're handled when they're very young kittens, that is. They do tend to pong a bit, but Meryl and Miriam say they won't mind that.'

It was good to have Fred there, talking about her family, especially about Miriam, her new step-mother, whom she loved so much, and intended to go on loving even though all the girls at school seemed to think that step-mothers had to be hated. Miriam was busy installing her model railway in the attic at Tŷ Corn Du. Fred had come to invite Simon over to help with it that evening. But now he couldn't, because he had to meet Dewi Llewelyn on the carn.

22

'Never mind,' Fred said. 'I'm home for a fortnight, remember. Surely he won't demand your constant attention for a fortnight!'

'He might,' Simon said. He was quite convinced that if there was anything irritating or inconvenient that Dewi *could* do, then it was certain that Dewi *would* do it.

Fred stayed for tea, and promised to come over again after school the next day to find out what had happened on the carn that evening. As Simon said goodbye to her, he wished that she was coming with him. He liked to have Fred with him. She did tend to nag a bit. But she was a good friend. And he had this awful feeling that something terrible might happen to him while he was with Dewi Llewelyn, alone.

3. A Talk in View of the Islands

Simon was looking at the Islands when Dewi rode up to the carn. He watched him as he slid from his pony, and sat down there with him. Then they looked at the Islands together.

After a while, Dewi sighed. 'So you can see them too, eh, Jones. Beautiful, aren't they?'

'Yes, ' Simon said. 'really beautiful. Look! There's the rainbow!' They watched, entranced, as the

23

rainbow formed, a perfect arc between the two tallest islands.

'See how the banners from the turrets on the castle match its colours.' Dewi was still smiling, and Simon realised that this was the first time he had ever seen him look really happy. 'I tell you what I'd like to do,' Dewi said with sudden infectious enthusiasm. 'I'd like to climb to the top of one of those towers and take one of those banners and bring it back and gallop all over the mountain at speed and have it streaming in the wind behind me.'

It was a wonderful idea. Simon laughed with the sheer joy of it, and Dewi laughed too, an excited shout of a laugh, lifting his chin and letting the wind from the Islands blow back his great dark mane of hair. 'Lets go there, Jones, me and you, and pinch a banner each. Bags I the purple one.'

'You can pinch one if you like,' Simon said. 'I'll do

it the easy way.I'll go and ask her if she'll give me one.'

'Ask her? Ask who?' Dewi turned sharply to look at him.

'The queen who lives out there,' Simon said. 'There's a queen, lives in the castle. Didn't you know?'

'No, I didn't know.' Dewi was scowling.

'I . . . I almost met her,' Simon said, 'last summer, when my friend, Fred, and I took the Unicorn to the other tall island, the one with the white beach and the cliff with the rhododendrons and the pine trees on it.'

Dewi's face had no expression at all on it now. 'Come again, Jones?' he said coldly.

'I'm not making it up', Simon said, and told him how he and Fred had found the Unicorn trapped on the mountain, and, with the Black Horn, had set it free on the tall, lonely island in the mist.

Dewi listened in icy silence. He was furious. When Simon had finished the story he said, bitterly: 'How is it that an incomer like you can have seen and done more on *my* mountain than I who was born here?'

Simon felt he should apologise, though he didn't see why. 'It seems to be my fate,' he said simply.

Dewi stared at him thoughtfully in the way he had been staring at school. 'You're Y Corn Du, aren't

25

you, Jones? You're the Wizard of the Black Horn,' he said. 'Mamgu said the new wizard was supposed to be here, but it wasn't until the day she died that I realised she meant you. Sitting up here, I was, and I looked down and seen your house, down below me on the mountain, and it came to me in a flash—that place is called Tŷ Corn Du Bach. It's Jones she means.'

'I saw you up here,' Simon told him.

'You never!' Dewi said scornfully. 'Not with your eyesight.'

Simon explained about the Black Horn. 'I . . . I saw her canhwyllau corff, too, that night she died,' he said.

Dewi glanced at him quickly, then looked away again. 'See the phantoms, did you?' he asked very casually.

'Yes,' Simon said.

'Nice, weren't they.' Dewi picked up a jagged piece of rock and threw it at a stonechat which was twittering on a gorse bush in front of them.

'Were they?' Simon wasn't sure if he meant it or if he was being sarcastic. He didn't know what to say. Should he tell him that they had been far from nice? 'I didn't actually look at them c-closely,' he stuttered as he lied. 'They were all hunched up. Were they p-people you knew?'

Dewi wouldn't look at him. He scowled at the

Islands. 'No. I never knew any of them. And I did see them close. I had to sing to them. Did you know that, Jones? Had to sing to phantoms, I did. They made me. And I'll never sing another note, so help me. Not another note. Never!' He threw another stone, at a sheep this time. It fled, bleating. 'Idiot!' he called out at it.

Simon felt acutely uncomfortable. It was an awful thing to have happened. He was horrified by it. But he didn't know what to say about it. And he had to say something. What? Talk about the grandmother again—that would be all right, perhaps. 'Your grandmother, your mamgu, she was complicated with magic like you are, wasn't she?' he said.

'Yeh!' Dewi looked proud. 'She could *do* things, Jones. Aw, the things she could do!' He frowned. 'She never had Second Sight, though. She never could see the Islands. Never understood why not, I couldn't—not that it mattered. She knew Old Blod, you know,' he said.

'Did she!' Simon was surprised, and annoyed too. 'Miss Emmanuel never mentioned her. Gosh, you'd think she would have told me that there was someone like your mamgu living over on the dark side of the mountain.'

Dewi glanced at him quickly again. He was smiling cynically. 'A perceptive little lad, aren't you, Jones bach,' he said.

27

'Perceptive about what?' Simon didn't know what he meant.

'The *dark* side of the mountain, you said,' Dewi told him, 'and that's certainly what it is, or what it feels like, any road—the dark side.' He swore softly in Welsh. 'Trust *you* to feel it. I suppose you can understand it, too. Can you? Can you understand *why* it feels so dark? And can you understand why it is that we Llewelyns should be fated to live in a dark place which isn't even fit for sheep or ponies? Can you tell me that, eh?' He sounded more bitter than ever.

'No,' Simon said. 'I can't tell you that. I don't know anything about you, or the dark side of the mountain. And I do think Miss Emmanuel could have told me all the things she knew.'

'See her often, do you?' Dewi asked.

'I go to see her every month,' Simon told him.

'What a good little sociable chap you are,' Dewi sniggered. 'Well, don't be too hard on the old faggot for not letting on about Mamgu,' he said. 'She was probably too terrified to tell you about her, see.'

'Blod? Terrified of your grandmother . . . ?' Simon was beginning to think that he would have to be very, very careful about anything which concerned Mamgu Llewelyn.

'Yeh!' Dewi grinned. 'Petrified of Mamgu, she was, I'll bet. Though, to be quite honest with you,

28

Jones, I know for a fact that she's petrified of you too.' He laughed rudely, but Simon had an idea that behind the laughter, Dewi was really quite surprised to think that unpleasant old Blod with her army of bees could be afraid of him.

He ignored the laughter. 'It was your grandmother who told you that, I suppose,' he said. 'Did she tell you what she thought about Miss Emmanuel being afraid of me?' he asked. 'Did it worry her?'

'Nah!' Dewi laughed scornfully now. 'But I don't mind telling you, Jones, it did make her sit up a bit,' he said frankly. 'She was inclined to dismiss you, though, bach, as being yet another one.'

'Yet another one of what?' Simon asked.

'Another one of the big con artists. We've had idiots on the mountain before under the illusion that they were the Second Wizard of Tŷ Corn Du, you know,' Dewi said. He was watching Simon carefully.

'I didn't know that,' Simon told him.

'Well we have, see,' Dewi said, 'so, naturally, Mamgu said here we go again, another idiot, and never bothered to check up on you. To be quite honest with you, Jones, she was ga-ga most of the time last year. Losing her grip, she was, or she'd have had a close look at you. I'm quite sure of that.'

Simon shivered. *He* was quite sure of that, too. He was thankful for Mamgu Llewelyn's senility.

Dewi was still looking at him thoughtfully. 'Jones, bach,' he said, 'there's something at our place I want you to come and have a look at. At least, my Mam wants you to come and have a look at it. Me and Da, well . . .' He pursed his lips and shook his head as he looked Simon up and down. 'Me and Da don't exactly share her confidence in your ability. But she wants you to come, so you might as well at least have a look at it.'

He was making fun of him again. Simon felt himself going very red. He tried to ignore it. 'What is it you want me to look at?' he asked.

Dewi glanced over his shoulder at the dark moor behind them. 'I won't talk about it up here, if you don't mind,' he said. 'One of the things Mamgu always dealt with, it is, see, and I don't feel too comfortable talking about that sort of thing in too much detail up here. So, come and have a look at it, Jones.' He stood up and called his pony. When it came, he vaulted onto its back, and sat there, looking down at Simon. 'After school tomorrow—come home with me, straight from the bus,' he said.

It was a command. He didn't ask. He didn't say 'Please will you come'. It was just 'Come!'

'Who does he think he is!' Simon felt irritated. 'Who does he think he is!'

4. The Dancers of the Moon

On his way back down the mountain, Simon remembered that Fred had promised to come over after school next day, but there was no point in her coming now, if he was going to go home with Dewi Llewelyn. He would have to phone Fred and tell her. He hoped that she wouldn't mind.

Fred didn't mind. She was too amazed and much too interested in it all to mind. 'You don't mean to say you've actually been invited to go to Castell Llewelyn?' she said. 'Brass bedknobs, Jonesy, nobody's ever invited there. This must be important.'

'Well, it wasn't exactly an invitation,' Simon said, 'it was more like an order—and yes, I'm afraid it must be because of something important.'

'Jonesy, you're not coming over all reluctant again, are you?' Fred said accusingly. 'And you've been so keen on magic and all that lately.'

'Oh, I'm still keen on magic,' Simon said. 'I'm not keen on Dewi Llewelyn, that's all.'

'Well, I must admit I don't blame you there. He is particularly horrid, isn't he. He buzzes me on that ghastly wild pony of his every time he sees me riding Gwenhwyfar on the mountain. And doesn't he show off about how well he can ride! And his father, that beastly, old Amahiah! He tells me off every time he sees me on the mountain. Anyone would think he owns the place. It amazes me how different *those* Llewelyns are from our Daniel. He was asking about you today, by the way ...' She stopped talking abruptly, and Simon heard her say 'Eh?' She seemed to be listening to someone else talking to her. She was. 'That was Guy,' she said. 'He told me not to forget you were paying for this call. Honestly, I swear he'd stand behind me with a stop-watch if Miriam would let him. But I'd better go, Jonesy. Tell you what, I'll phone you tomorrow. Then you can tell me all about Castell Llewelyn and that. I'll be dying to hear all day. I only wish I was going to be there too,' Fred said, and, next day, as he walked with Dewi on the dark side of the mountain, Simon, too, wished fervently that Fred was there. The darkness was terrible.

The sun shone, but still the darkness was terrible. It was an odd darkness, more of a feeling of darkness in his mind than real darkness. Simon tried to analyse the feeling. It was a sort of apprehension, a tension in the air, as though a storm was all around and, at any moment, could break. He felt his heart thumping. He wanted to run, to run right away, but he clenched his fists and made himself breathe steadily, and walked along quietly beside Dewi, who was also quiet. And then, suddenly, they came to a stone circle.

Dewi, of course, knew that the circle was there. He also knew that Simon didn't know about it, but he didn't warn him. It was hidden from the path by a fold in the mountain which made the track curve around a blind corner. Dewi had obviously planned that Simon would walk around that corner and find himself right up against the circle almost before he realised that it was there. He had obviously planned to frighten him.

But Simon wasn't frightened. He did realise that Dewi expected him to be frightened, and he realised, too, that Dewi was amazed that he wasn't, for Dewi himself was terrified of the stones.

'Now, why is he so afraid of them?' Simon wondered. As far as he could see and feel there was nothing whatsoever to be afraid of in those stones. The darkness was terrifying, yes, but the stone circle—well, *that* felt wonderful—wonderful and fascinating. And didn't it look interesting too!

There were twelve tall stones in the circle, and a lot of short, round stones. The tall stones were upright and grey, and were set in what he was sure must be a perfect circle. They were spaced evenly, with long gaps of equal length between them which were divided into four shorter, equal gaps by the small, round stones.

'This is a clock,' Simon thought. He stood still and let his mind feel it. It was strange, but, no, it wasn't frightening. 'So why is Dewi scared of it?' he wondered again. He began to watch Dewi carefully. Yes, he was most certainly terrified of those stones. He decided to ask him about them, and then he discovered that Dewi thought of the stones as people. He didn't know anything about them, but he thought of them as people and he knew their name.

'They're "Y Dawnswyr y Lleuad", the Dancers of the Moon,' he told Simon. 'Got to have respect for them, Mamgu said. Told me not to go near them, never.'

'Are they what you've brought me to see?' Simon asked.

'Nope!' Dewi said. 'Interesting and gruesome though they are, it's not them. They're just a bit of history to be avoided, Mamgu said. No, come on, it's indoors.'

Simon was fascinated with Castell Llewelyn. It was just a farm now, but, once, it had really been a castle. Its walls were much thicker than the walls of a normal, old house, and some of its windows were as small as arrow slits, and, on the corner of the main building, he noticed that they passed what could only have been the ruins of a very large tower.

Dewi took him to the front door. There was a porch there, which, although it was old, was much newer than the rest of the house. 'We generally go round the back,' Dewi told him, 'but Mam said I was

34

to bring you to the front.' He sneered. 'It's not every day we get crachach visitors all the way from Petts Wood,' he said.

Simon ignored him, but he couldn't ignore the young sheep-dog which came hurtling around the side of the house, not to be deprived of a good bark and a growl just because someone had been misguided enough to use the wrong door.

'Iste, Brenin!' Dewi spoke to him in Welsh. Simon knew the word 'brenin'. The dog was called King, and, when Dewi opened the door to the porch, there was another Brenin there, an old dog, semi-retired, asleep where it was warm.

'Two dogs called Brenin?' Simon said.

'Yep, we always called our dogs Brenin,' Dewi told him. Simon would have loved to ask why, but didn't like to.

Dewi's mother and father were sitting at the table in the middle of one of the biggest and cleanest kitchens that Simon had ever seen. They seemed to be there especially to meet him, for as soon as he had shaken hands with them they went out and got on with their work.

Dewi's mother was a pleasant, plump woman, with short, dark, crinkly hair. She smiled at Simon shyly, and he had a feeling that she was a little flustered, as though she felt she was meeting someone important. He was embarrassed, but he liked her.

Amahiah, however, he did not like. He looked all beak, with his hooked, bony nose. 'Like a vulture,' Simon thought. 'And he wears his cap indoors! And that stare!' Amahiah's look was far more cold than anything Simon had had to suffer from Dewi. No, Simon did not like Amahiah. He was glad when he went and left them.

'Leave your satchel here, Jones bach,' Dewi said. 'Now, let me see, the best bit was in the bathroom cupboard this morning. Mam!' he called. 'Did you leave it, like I said?'

'Yes,' his mother called from the scullery. 'I left it. But don't you leave it now, Dewi. You promised. As soon as the boy had seen it . . .'

'All right, all right!' Dewi said impatiently. He picked up a short, sharp, shining sickle. 'I won't leave it,' he said. He looked at Simon and laughed. 'You look as though you think you've come to the mad-house, Jones,' he said. 'Well, to be quite honest with you, it's rapidly turning into one. Come on now!'

Dewi opened a door at the side of the kitchen, yelled something in Welsh which sounded like a war-cry, and ran, leaping two at a time, up the steep, stone stairway which was shut away behind the door. 'First left—the bathroom,' he shouted, 'and

Mam's nice airing cupboard, warm as a greenhouse.' He stopped in the doorway. 'And, Duw, it's thrived in there all right?' he said.

Simon peered over Dewi's shoulder. There, twining out through the not-quite-closed airing-cupboard door, was what Dewi had brought him to see. It was a dark green, poisonous-looking vine.

5. The Dark Green Vine

Dewi had yelled a war cry. Now he leapt into battle. He attacked. The gleaming sickle sliced through the air—and the vine avoided it. The vine moved. It lunged. It reached. The vine fought back.

Simon stood quite still, his back against the wall. He couldn't believe it. It was a trick. It wasn't happening. It was the movement of the air. Vines didn't fight. Vines *couldn't* fight. But this vine could and it did, though it didn't win. He watched until, cut through, it lay limp upon the floor. Then, cautiously, he stepped forward and bent to look at it.

'Don't touch!' Dewi said. 'Watch!'

Simon jerked back and watched again, and soon he was retreating, stepping quickly out of the room, as the cut tendril of the plant began to writhe like an animal which had been mortally wounded. It was horrible. He looked away from it and saw the cut stem hanging from the cupboard door. It was dripping blood. He began to feel sick.

Dewi was still excited. 'There he goes!' he shouted, and lashed out again with the sickle as the vine retreated, pulling itself back into the cupboard. Quickly, Simon looked down at the tendril again. Now that was beginning to disintegrate, to turn to dust and fine, white ashes. It was magic. Of course it was. All of it. But *whose* magic? He began to feel very frightened.

And now, strangely, Dewi who had been terrified of the stone circle wasn't at all scared of this. He scuffed at the dust on the floor with the toe of his shoe, then flung open the cupboard door. 'Look!' he said, and Simon was just in time to see the end of the vine, still dripping blood, disappear back into the wall of the farmhouse. 'That thing's invading us,' Dewi told him. 'The cellar's full of it. It's breaking up the walls. And every day it breaks out in a different cupboard. Now *that's* what I brought you to see, Jones. What do you think of *that*, eh?'

'I think it's ghastly,' Simon said, 'and I suppose you expect me to be able to get rid of it.'

Dewi sneered. 'Not *expect*, Mr Corn Du from Petts Wood. *Hope*. Hope is the word. Come on in to my room and I'll tell you all about it.'

Simon wasn't surprised to see that Dewi's bedroom window looked out on to the carn. He didn't have a good, clear view of it though. It was half hidden for him by a rise in the moorland, and overshadowed, somehow, by the Dancers of the Moon.

But, although the view from the room wasn't surprising, the room itself was. Standing in it was like standing on top of the mountain. Its walls and its ceiling were covered with a mural of the view from the carn. Not the ordinary view, but the magic view, the view which could only be seen by someone with Second Sight, for, though the ceiling was filled with clouds and birds, and three walls were mountain and moorland, the fourth wall, which ordinarily would have been sea with nothing but a few bright sails upon its surface, the fourth wall held the Islands in all their mysterious glory.

Simon smiled with sheer joy when he saw them. 'Hey! That's great! Who did it?' he asked. 'Not you!'

'Who do you think did it, idiot, some incomer from the town? Second Sight comes two-a-penny these days, does it then?'

'But I didn't even know that you could draw.' Simon stared at the painting incredulously. 'You don't do things like this in school.'

'You're dead right I don't do things like this in

school. I reckon they know enough about me in school without me letting on about this.'

'But how can you hide being able to draw like this?'

'Jones bach, a Llewelyn can hide anything if he tries hard enough,' Dewi bragged. 'Now, you'd better make yourself comfy, like. Mam wants to bring us up some tea. I'll give her a shout.' He went out and leant over the rail at the top of the stairs and called to his mother, and Simon sat down where he could look at the painting of the Islands. Then, as soon as Mrs Llewelyn had gone back downstairs, Dewi explained about the vine. At least, he thought he was explaining about it, but Simon found that the more he heard of what Dewi had to say, the more muddled he became. In fact, there was only one piece of information in the whole of Dewi's explanation which he felt he could believe, and that was that the Llewelyns of Castell Llewelyn were the Kings of the Mountain.

'Da says it's a guy called O'Shaughnessy who's making this vine grow,' Dewi began. 'He was one of the con men Mamgu told me about. He came here and turned real evil when he found *us* here, the Kings of the Mountain.'

'Eh?' Simon interrupted him. 'What did you say— the Kings of the Mountain?'

'Yeh!' Dewi sneered. 'You never knew that, did

you? Thought it might surprise you, I did. Yeh, we've been Kings of the Mountain since time immemorial, Jones,' he said.

'So that's why your farm is a castle and you call your dogs Brenin.'

'Yeh, obvious when you know, isn't it! But let me not bore you with my obvious superiority, you poor, under-privileged citizen of Petts Wood. Let me get back to this guy, O'Shaughnessy. Can you concentrate on O'Shaughnessy again, Jones, or are you still reeling from the shock of me being king of this mountain you like to think is yours?'

'Bighead!' Simon thought, but he didn't say anything.

'Well,' Dewi went on, 'O'Shaughnessy came here and tried to convince Mamgu that he was the Second Wizard of Tŷ Corn Du, or some such nonsense. Told me all about it, Mamgu did. A right idiot he was, useless at magic, she said. Came here making trouble, pretending to be cleverer than she was, and then turned real nasty when she threw him off the mountain and told him to go back to where he belonged. Vowed revenge on her, he did. That's what Mamgu said. And Da says that's what this vine is—O'Shaughnessy's way of getting his own back.

'He's tried it before, see. Time and again he's made it grow, but she's always managed to keep it

41

off. Only now she's not here, now he's managing to get his own back on us.'

'So he is a wizard of some sort, then, even if he isn't the one he pretended to be,' Simon said. 'But why does he want to get his own back on you now that she's gone? And why doesn't he just come back himself now that she's not here to throw him out? Is he still afraid of something or someone?'

'No, no! Idiot! You're getting it all wrong,' Dewi sounded exasperated. 'O'Shaughnessy wasn't a wizard. Mamgu said he wasn't. And he's dead now, see. He must be. He was an old man when he came here when Da was younger than me. Died donkey's years ago, he must have. But Da says it's him who's sending the vine.'

'How does he know that?'

Dewi scowled. 'He won't say. There's a lot of things Da won't say. Keeps things from me, he does. But if he says it's O'Shaughnessy, then it's O'Shaughnessy. You can count on that.'

Simon sipped his tea. It didn't make sense. A man called O'Shaughnessy who wasn't a wizard was sending this animal vine to invade the farm so that he could have some sort of revenge on Mamgu Llewelyn, even though she was dead and so was he. It was rubbish. Dewi was talking rubbish. He wondered if he dared tell him, and decided that he didn't dare. 'What exactly do you hope I can do?' he asked carefully. It seemed the safest thing to say.

'Get rid of the vine, of course, idiot,' Dewi said.

Simon put down his cup. 'All right,' he said. 'I'll have a go. But I've no idea how to do it at the moment, so it might take a while. I'll have to look up a few things.'

'Can't you just blast it with that horn you've got?' Dewi said impatiently. 'Blod told Mamgu you were pretty deadly with that horn. Petrified of it she was, Mamgu said. Talked of lightning striking and stones shattering. So come and blast O'Shaughnessy's vine. That's what we want.'

So that was it! That was why they had brought him here. Blod had been talking about the things he could do with the Black Horn, and now they thought all they had to do was bring him here and tell him to get on and use it. He sat looking at Dewi. 'Wretched Kings of the Mountain!' he thought. 'Do this, do that! Well, I'm not going to.' He knew that, sooner or later, he was going to have to stand up to Dewi, to say definitely no, or the flow of orders and commands would never stop. 'I suppose I'd better start now,' he thought, and resigned himself to a tirade of rudeness and abuse. 'No!' he said, as firmly as he could. 'I won't blast the vine for you.'

Dewi scowled. 'Why not?'

43

'Because I don't like using the Horn like that. It—it isn't necessary.'

'Afraid of using it like that, are you?' Dewi was sneering again. 'Or doesn't the little lad want to kill the poor old vine then?' he asked in an exaggerated babyish voice.

'That's about it,' Simon said, trying not to let Dewi upset him. 'I don't like things being killed, and I hope I never have to kill anything myself, ever, especially not with the Horn. The Horn shouldn't be used like that. Well, only when I can't help it, I suppose. But really it's meant for me to use—to *work* with. The power I have is meant to be worked with, not fought with.'

Dewi looked right through him. 'Jones,' he said, 'not only are you an idiot, you are also a prat—a goody-goody, crachach, minuscule prat. And here I am stuck with you. What is the mountain coming to!' He sighed and shook his head in mock despair. 'OK, I give in, no blasting. So, what do you propose to do instead?'

Simon knew that Dewi hadn't given in. This was only the beginning of the argument. He tried to think. 'Well, there must be some other way of getting rid of the vine,' he said. 'How did your grandmother keep it off? Do you know?'

'Nope! I don't know a lot about any of the things she did. Kept that all to herself, did Mamgu.' Dewi pretended to think carefully. 'But she did say something, once, about a cupful of little flowers,' he said.

'Perhaps I could use them too. What sort of flowers were they, do you know that?'

Dewi laughed. 'No, I don't know that, and nobody else does neither. Mamgu never told her secrets, Jones. You might as well give up trying to follow that line right away.' He laughed again. 'You're going to *have* to use that Black Horn,' he said. 'You'll learn that you might as well save your breath when you fancy arguing with one of us. We Kings of the Mountain always get our way. You'll be blasting old O'Shaughnessy's vine, you'll see, just like I said.'

Simon found himself hating Dewi more than he had ever hated him before. He stood up, rather stiffly and awkwardly. 'I'm sorry,' he said, 'but I'm not going to blast the vine. I'll get rid of it for you in my own way, or I won't get rid of it at all.'

Dewi refused to take him seriously. 'Give over arguing, Jones. You might as well. Like I said, we Kings . . .'

'I'm sorry.' Simon stood there stubbornly. 'I must do it my own way.' For a moment he thought that Dewi was going to hit him. Perhaps he would have, but he never did, for, at that moment, Mrs Llewelyn screamed.

It was terrible scream, a choking cry, a shriek of terror. Instantly, Dewi forgot Simon. He snatched up the sickle and leapt towards the stairway. Simon rushed after him.

They found her huddled against a cupboard in her kitchen, with the vine twining tightly around her throat. Dewi tore it away from her. Then he hacked at it, chopping and slashing at it until Simon thought he must have gone berserk.

And Mrs Llewelyn cried. She cried and begged and

pleaded with Simon. 'Please, *please,* if you *are* Corn Du, please, if you *can* get rid of this awful thing, please do it. It's me it'll get. It's *me*, I'm here all day. They're off out of it. It's me it'll get . . .'

Simon couldn't bear it. He couldn't bear to look at her. He turned away from her and stumbled across the kitchen. He must get out! He must get away. He found a door and wrenched it open. He half fell through. But he wasn't outside. He was in the scullery. Frantically, he peered around, looking for another door.

He *felt* the Cauldron. He didn't see it. He felt it. It stood, out of the way, at one end of the scullery. It stood in darkness. It held darkness. It *was* darkness—the same menacing darkness which lay across the moorland.

Simon shuddered. He stood there, feeling it with his mind. And that part of his mind which knew about magic was telling him, warning him, that he was standing in the presence of something more evil than anything he would ever meet again in his whole life.

6. Simon Begins to Sort Things Out

Dewi came as far as the Dancers of the Moon with Simon. He had wanted to ride with him as far as the carn, but Amahiah wouldn't let him. They had argued in Welsh, something about work and horses, and Dewi had explained. 'He says I've got to get on with my chores. What he really means is he doesn't want me skiving off up there looking at those Islands. I'm supposed to avert mine eyes from such things, like he does, see. So I think, little lad, that you had better not go home that way on your own. Take the path around the mountain, not over. You might dodge the worst of the darkness that way, if you're quick.'

But Simon hadn't been quick enough. The darkness gathered. He could feel it gathering. He felt that it was looking at him, feeling that he was there. He hurried. He didn't run. Running would be a mistake. He hurried. He was glad when he saw the lights of the town ahead of him. Then, and only then, could he relax and think.

He thought about the Cauldron, that awful Cauldron. He wanted to shudder every time he remembered it. What could there be about it that made him so certain that here was evil?

He had asked Dewi about it, but all that Dewi could tell him was that it was Mamgu's cauldron. He seemed quite proud of it, but, of course, he would be. He was very proud of everything his grandmother could do, it seemed, and everything she said, too. 'Which makes *him* the idiot,' Simon thought, 'for, if that's *her* cauldron then she was nothing to be proud of. She was awful—terrible.'

He walked along thinking about Mamgu and the Cauldron and the darkness. Then he began to think about all the things she had told Dewi about the vine and O'Shaughnessy, and he realised that everything she had told him was completely unbelievable. None of it made sense. 'She told him a pack of lies!' Simon felt quite shocked when he realised this. 'Why ever would she want to tell him lies?' He couldn't understand it.

He thought about it all a little longer, and finally decided that he wasn't going to believe any of the things Mamgu had told Dewi, except that there had been a man called O'Shaughnessy who came to the mountain, and that it was O'Shaughnessy who was making the vine invade Castell Llewelyn. 'Amahiah said that that was true, and I think it's safe to believe what *he* says,' he thought. 'But who was O'Shaughnessy? And was he a wizard? He must have been. But why is he making the vine grow?'

There was so much he needed to find out, so many questions unanswered. He would have to find out more and more and more. But who could he ask? Where could he look?

As far as he could see there were two possibilities. One was—he could go and ask Miss Emmanuel. The other was—he could try to find the answers in *The Myddfai Historian*. 'Blod will probably know it all, but I bet she won't tell me any of it,' he thought. 'She'll still be afraid of Mamgu even though she's dead—and no wonder. She was terrible—and there are too many things happening around here after people are dead. No, I won't ask Blod. I'll try *The Historian*.'

As he walked in through the kitchen door his mother called from her conservatory. 'Fred has phoned three times,' she told him. 'She says not to phone her as she's going out. She'll phone again as soon as she gets in.'

'*Three* times! O dear!' Simon thought. Fred must be very enthusiastic about something to have phoned him three times. 'She wants to nag me,' he thought. 'She wants to make me *do* something. Oh dear!' He called back to his mother. 'Did she say what she wanted to talk to me about?'

'No,' Mother called, 'but it sounded important.' Simon began to feel apprehensive. Then he felt guilty about feeling apprehensive. Fred was such a bother to him. She only wanted to help, and he was very glad of her company at times. But she did make him do things he didn't want to do, and she did *nag*.

He went upstairs to his room. It was no good worrying about Fred. He had enough to worry about already, with poor Mrs Llewelyn and this vine, and Dewi being King of the Mountain. And who was this man, O'Shaughnessy? He took down *The Myddfai Historian* from its place on top of his wardrobe, dusted it with his sleeve, and sat on his window sill, and read.

The Myddfai Historian was a book of magic. It was heavy, with a black, leather cover and nine hundred and ninety-nine pages covered with very small handwritten print. He thought of it as his magic manual. His mother had hundreds of gardening manuals to help her in her work, and his father had almost as many manuals on sailing. Simon had just one, *The Myddfai Historian*.

He knew that he ought to read *The Historian* regularly. When he first had it he had made a habit of reading a page or two nearly every day, but it hurt his eyes to read the small letters, and he soon gave it up and just looked up things he wanted to know when he needed to know them. There was an index. 'What should I look up?' he wondered now. What did he want to know about? 'Mamgu Llewelyn,' he thought, and found 'Llewelyn' in the index.

Eagerly, he turned to the right page. It was about Llewelyn Fawr, a great prince of Wales. It mentioned Snowdonia and castles in the North, but there was nothing about Castell Llewelyn and this mountain at all.

He decided to look up 'darkness' instead. It wasn't in the index. Next he tried 'cauldron'. There were no less than twelve references to cauldrons. As he looked for the first of these his eyes began to sting and water.

It was hopeless. He shut *The Historian*. It was absolutely hopeless. 'Blast my eyes!' he thought. 'Blast everything!' He looked up at the carn; he couldn't even see that properly tonight. The moon was completely hidden. The sky above the carn seemed as thick as soup. But there was moonlight on the side of the mountain.

It was odd. Why were there only patches of moonlight? It wasn't because of clouds. There were no clouds, as far as he could tell. So, why was there only moonlight on the side of the mountain and, yes, just a small patch on the carn, and then no moonlight at all?

Simon guessed the answer. 'The moonlight stops where the dark side of the mountain begins,' he thought. 'The darkness, the Cauldron darkness, shuts out the moonlight.' Was this significant, he wondered. Then he wondered if perhaps he was imagining it all. Perhaps it was just because of his wretched eyes that he couldn't see the moonlight, and he reached out and picked up the Black Horn.

And then, something completely unexpected happened. As his hand touched the Black Horn, the very moment it touched it, magic began. *The Myddfai Historian,* which lay closed on his lap, fell open with a snap—and quietly and gently, one by one, its pages began to turn.

7. The Myddfai Historian

The pages of *The Historian* turned. They turned and they turned, gently, gently, silently, silently. It was as though a hand which he couldn't see was searching, quietly and thoroughly, for a passage, a reference, a clue. Simon let go of the book so quickly that it almost fell from his lap to the floor. Immediately, the pages lay still.

He sat, afraid to move, not daring to look around. Who was doing it? Who was in the room with him? He listened, feeling with his mind.

There was no one there, nothing. Gradually he relaxed. He was alone in the room. There was just him, the Black Horn, and *The Myddfai Historian.* He began to wonder. Had he just discovered something else that he could do with the Black Horn in his hands?

He decided to experiment. Carefully, he reached out and laid his left hand on the edge of the open book. He was frightened. His hand wouldn't stop shaking. He pressed it against the warm leather, making it lie still, and gripped the Black Horn with his right hand. Immediately, the pages began to turn again. To and fro they went, haphazardly, to and fro.

'It *is* me!' That was definite. He stopped feeling frightened. This was good! This was marvellous! He could make the pages turn themselves. Now, what could he do with this? Look things up, of course! it was the obvious answer. But how could he make it work sensibly? The pages were just flicking over and over. That was no good at all. 'Perhaps I have to *ask The Historian* to show me what I want to know,' he thought. 'Yes, that could be the way to use this. But how do I ask it?' He wondered about this for a while, and decided that he must simply have to *think* about whatever it was that he wanted to know about. So— what did he want to know about? He decided to begin with the Llewelyns again.

He was beginning to feel quite excited. 'The Llewelyns who live on the dark side of this mountain.' He sat still, gripping the Black Horn and thinking, thinking, carefully, about the dark side of the mountain. He imagined it. He remembered how it looked. And he thought of Dewi.

The pages of *The Historian* began to turn again,

more definitely now, more purposefully. There was nothing frantic or urgent about their movement. There was nothing to be frightened of. In fact, as he watched it, the movement of the pages made him relax, and he stared at it, half mesmerised, until it stopped, and *The Historian* lay open and still again. Then he put down the Black Horn, held the book close to his eyes, and began to read. *'Onne ye moone sydde of ye mountaine,'* he read.

He stopped reading. 'On the *moon* side of the mountain, not the *dark* side—the *moon* side. So I'm not imagining things about the moon. It *is* involved. On the moon side of the mountain . . .' He thought of moonlight, mysterious, silver and beautiful. That was how the moor should be. It shouldn't be covered with darkness. The darkness didn't belong there at all. He began to read again:

'Onne ye moone sydde of ye mountaine, there lyethe ye dwellynge which do belonge to ye Kinges of ye Mountaine, ye famillie Llewelyn.' So that *was* true. He had been right to believe that. Now, what else had he been right or wrong about? Simon read on, his interest and excitement growing with every word he read.

He read that the Llewelyn family were said to be very distantly related to Llewelyn Fawr, but that they had never cared to claim to be princes of Wales. They were content to be the Kings of the Mountain.

He read, too, that the Llewelyns owned a wonderful crown which was thought to be a circle of gold decorated with the moon and the stars, but that the writer had never actually seen it, nor had he been able to find anyone else who had seen it. He said it was: *'ye Secrette keppte close by ye Llewelynnes'*, and he said, too, that in his opinion the crown was precious to the Llewelyns not because of its value in gold or jewels, but because it has been given to them by *'certainee elven folke'* as a sign that they would remain the Kings of the Mountain for ever.

'Itte is also told,' Simon read, *'that ye crowne do be importante in certainne ceremonies which ye Llewelynnes do perform in grette voyce. These ceremonies do takke place within a certainne circle of Stonnes ycleppte Dawnswyr y Lleuad or Ye Dancers of ye Moone. This circle do Stonde cloSe by ye CaStell Llewelyn one ye Moone Syde of ye Mountainne. And it do be rumoured also that ye Llewelyns with their muSicke and their crowne do verily makke ye Dancers to Dance.'*

Simon closed the book. 'The Dancers of the Moon,' he thought. 'The Llewelyns can make the Dancers dance—make those huge stones *move*. Gosh!' Suddenly, he remembered Dewi walking beside the stone circle. Dewi wouldn't be able to make those stones move. Dewi wouldn't go near enough to try. Dewi was terrified of them.

Simon sat there, remembering what Dewi had said

about the stone circle. He had said that it was interesting but gruesome and something to be avoided. 'He said that his grandmother had told him that they were dangerous. He said that she had told him always to keep away from them. All *that* was lies too. But why ever would she tell him all those lies?' Simon couldn't understand it at all.

He began to think about Mamgu Llewelyn again. He still had to find out about Mamgu, but it would be no good looking in *The Historian* for her. *The Historian* had been written hundreds of years before she was born.

He looked up at the carn again. The moon was there, the crescent moon, high above the grey shadow of the stones. For a few seconds, no more, it raced above the dark mass that was the mountain, then it was gone again, swallowed by darkness.

'And there shouldn't be darkness, not *that* darkness—it's the moon's side, over there, the moon's side,' he thought. 'Why is there no moon on the moon's side?'

It had to be because of Mamgu—Mamgu and her Cauldron. The Cauldron and the darkness felt exactly the same, so it followed that Mamgu had somehow made, or brought, the darkness with her Cauldron.

'But where does this man O'Shaughnessy come into it?' He had to find out about O'Shaughnessy

57

and his vine, too. He tapped the cover of *The Historian*. 'He won't be in here either,' he thought. 'I'll have to find out about him somewhere else, and I'll have to find out about Mamgu and that Cauldron somewhere else—and, gosh!' He suddenly realised something which he felt must be important. 'Dewi never even mentioned that there was a crown.'

The more Simon thought about this, the more he was convinced that it was significant. 'He never said a word about it. Not one single, bragging, big-headed word. And if ever there was something to be big-headed about it would be that crown.' It could only mean one thing. 'He doesn't know about it. He doesn't know they've got a crown. Mamgu never ever told him about it—nor did Amahiah.'

Downstairs, the telephone buzzed, 'Fred!' Simon groaned. 'Fred nagging like mad.'

'That'll be Fred,' his mother called as she went to answer it. He heard her say; 'Hello, Fred, I thought it must be you. Yes, he's here now. Hold on. It is Fred,' she called. 'Take it in my room.'

He went into his mother's room and sat on her pink and white bedspread and prepared to withstand the onslaught of Fred's enthusiasm.

'Jonesy!' Fred said. 'Don't say anything. Just listen and then tell me if I'm right. Are you listening?'

'Yes,' Simon said.

'Right! When you got to Castell Llewelyn tonight,

58

you found that what they wanted you to do was to get rid of a beastly, magic vine. Now, is that right, or is it not right?'

'It's right.' Simon was amazed. 'But how did you find out?'

'Daniel told me. He knew a man called O'Shaughnessy who used to live there once. He was a bit of a dyn hysbys, this O'Shaughnessy. He told Daniel that he would send that vine especially to make sure that when the new Wizard of the Black Horn came along he would have to take a special interest in Castell Llewelyn ... Jonesy, Daniel wants to talk to you.'

8. O'Shaughnessy's Friend Daniel

Simon ran downstairs. If he didn't see Daniel tonight he would have to wait until after school tomorrow, and that would be a whole day wasted, and another whole day for poor Mrs Llewelyn to be suffering that vine. He mustn't forget poor Mrs Llewelyn.

'I've got to go to see a man Fred knows,' he told his mother.

'Do I know him?'

'I expect so. He's a gardener ...'

'Oh, Daniel!'

'Yes. He's waiting over at Tŷ Corn Du to see me. I'll take my bike. I won't be long.'

'But it's bedtime. It's school tomorrow,' his mother began to protest.

'And the battery in your rear light's flat,' his father said.

'There! You can't possibly go.' His mother sounded relieved.

But his father was picking up his car keys. 'You can't possibly go on your bike,' he said. 'I'll take you. Come on, Dil, you'd better come too, or you'll have had kittens by the time we get back. We can make an evening of it, with Meryl and Smithy and Miriam and Guy, while we're waiting.'

The summer was over, the tourists had gone home, they didn't meet one single car on the road to Tŷ Corn Du. 'Nice and quick!' Dad said. 'Not quite like magic, but a good second best, I think.' He realised that Simon was busy with something special, and Simon understood exactly why he was making silly jokes. It was because his mother knew that he was busy, too, and his mother had to be kept cheerful. She was looking at him, now, in the way that she looked when she knew that he was being the Wizard of the Black Horn, and wasn't sure if he was still the same Simon who had only been her son.

Simon was glad when Fred came running out to meet them, with Meryl just behind her.

'Oh good!' Meryl said. 'I was hoping you would come too, Dil. I want to pick your brains. It's about the ha-ha beyond the avenue.'

'Come on!' Fred pulled Simon away from them. 'Daniel's in the summer house. Do you know, Jonesy, he just loves the summer house. He knows it's special and magic. He's insisting that nobody does anything whatsoever to change it. Guy was keen to tidy it up, you see, but Daniel told him off. All he'll let them do is make new steps and strengthen the floor a bit.'

'That's good,' Simon said. 'It shouldn't be interfered with, I'm sure it shouldn't.'

'That's what Daniel said.' Fred nodded enthusiastically. 'I think, you know, that although he's not actually one of those king-type Llewelyns up there on the mountain, just being a cousin must make him a bit fey or something.'

'What's he like?' Simon began to feel nervous. What if this old man was like the dreadful Amahiah? 'Is he nice?' he asked.

'Yes . . . Ssh!' Fred whispered. 'He's not at all deaf, even though he's seventy-two.'

'Seventy-three!' Daniel corrected her from somewhere behind the rose-hips and fading leaves which were draped across the summer house like

61

some voluminous red and yellow curtain. He was smoking. Next moment they seemed to be engulfed in a cloud of tobacco smoke. It smelt, vaguely, of chrysanthemums. 'Seventy-three years old I am, and next St David's Day, God willing, I'll be seventy-four.'

'Will you really!' Someone had leant a short ladder against the side of the summer house, the sort with wide, firm steps—much safer than the old, rotting, built-in stairway. Fred scampered up them, talking eagerly. 'On St David's Day, too. That's special isn't it.'

'It is for me,' Daniel said. 'Now, where's this Jonesy, then? Where's this young lad who has taken the Black Horn down from the wall of Tŷ Corn Du and kept it for his own?'

'Here he is, 'Fred said. 'Come on, Jonesy. He won't eat you.'

Daniel Llewelyn laughed, and was still chuckling as Simon made his way up the steps and stood in front of him. All Simon could see of him was a bulky shadow and a glowing pipe bowl.

'No, I won't eat you,' Daniel said. 'It was O'Shaughnessy they said would eat all comers, not me. That was how they billed him, see.'

'Billed him?' Fred asked.

'Yes, billed him. You know what I mean—advertised him on the bills and posters they stuck up to say he was going to be fighting.'

'Fighting?' Simon didn't like the sound of that.

'Yes, fighting. O'Shaughnessy was a wrestler, see,' Daniel said. 'He was something else besides a wrestler, but not everybody knew about that. To folk around here, he was a wrestler.' He drew an imaginary poster in the air. 'O'Shaughnessy, the Irish Giant. Always Goes Down Fighting. ' He chuckled again. 'Fighting and singing, that's what he was famous for.' He cleared his throat and began to sing, conducting himself with his pipe. The bowl glowed red in the darkness of the summer house. To and fro, it went, trailing sparks, like a small comet which had lost its true orbit.

> *'Fight and sing. Beat the drums.*
> *See, Fianna's warrior comes.*
> *Sing and fight. Who will dare?*
> *O'Shaughnessy, the man of Eire.'*

'I think that last word was E-I-R-E, seeing he was Irish,' Daniel said, 'but it could have been A-I-R, him being what he was. I never saw the word written down, you see, only heard it being sung. Used to come along singing it, he did, and soon we'd all be joining in with him. Ah, those old days . . . In our prime, we were. *I* was, any road. O'Shaughnessy, well, he was getting on a bit, I think. Though to be quite honest with you I never could tell how old he was, exactly. Difficult to judge, age was in him. Still strong as an ox, he was. Indeed yes, a great Irish ox.' He chuckled again, and then stuck his pipe in his mouth and sucked at it with noisy smackings of his lips.

'He was a dyn hysbys, wasn't he?' Fred prompted Daniel. 'Everybody thought he was just a travelling wrestler, but you knew differently, didn't you. He told *you* the truth about himself, didn't he?'

'Indeed he did. Some of it, any road.' Daniel had found an old armchair for himself, and a packing case to use as a table. He was very comfortable. 'You had better settle down somewhere. Take the weight off your legs. This will take some telling, young Jones,' he said.

'That's all right,' Simon said. He sat down, cross-legged, on the floor in front of Daniel. 'It doesn't matter how long it takes. I'd like to hear everything you can remember, please. I need to know it all.'

'We'll be OK here till midnight, I should think.' Fred had propped herself against one of the more reliable trellis posts which supported the roses and creepers. 'Once they start talking Tŷ Corn Du garden they go on all night.'

'And quite right too,' Daniel said. 'Any other time and I would be tempted to join them. But tonight, I must tell this young man about O'Shaughnessy.'

He struck a match, and he and Simon looked at each other, briefly, as it flared. Then he pressed it against the bowl of his pipe and sucked at it until the tobacco glowed brightly again. He was a big man, Simon saw. His shoulders, though stooping now, were still broad, and his hands were enormous. He had the Llewelyn nose, too, Simon noticed, though his was broader than Amahiah's, and more in keeping with his size.

When he was satisfied with the state of his pipe, he began to talk again. 'O'Shaughnessy came from nowhere,' he told Simon. 'Any road, that was how it seemed. Nobody saw him come, and nobody saw him go, neither. He had a path he knew, you see. It was a way, a secret way, he told me, but he wouldn't say where it was or where it went. All I know about it is that it brought him out on to the mountain. And that was where he came one night, suddenly. He appeared among them up there, or so my uncle said.'

'Which one was your uncle?' Simon wanted to get this straight. There were so many Llewelyns.

'Old Llewelyn, Dewi's grandfather, him who was father to Amahiah. Him who *she* came to marry.'

Simon knew who 'she' must be. 'Did you know her, Dewi's grandmother, Mamgu?' he asked. 'Did you meet her? What was she like?'

'Steady on, bach!' Daniel said. 'One question at a time. Did I meet her? Yes, I did. Did I know her? No, I did not. I doubt if anybody really knew her, or would ever want to know her, once they'd met her. For, what was she like? She was wicked, Jones, wicked and evil and cunning. There was no telling how cunning she should be. Ah, she was *bad*.

'She came to the mountain to set her cap at my uncle—not because she loved him, oh no! She was incapable of love. It was because she coveted the crown that she came. She wanted that crown. The crown of the Kings of the Mountain. And she soon got it, too. Off his head and on to her own it went, as soon as she had him where she wanted him.

'He was a weak man, you see, Jones. Some men are weak. Amahiah is weak, too, even though he's nasty. This boy of his, though, this Dewi, now he, Jones, he has the making of not being weak. But you will know that if you have met him.'

'Yes,' Simon said. 'He's not weak. He's—he's not nice either.'

'The Kings of the Mountain never are,' Daniel said. 'Even though they are my kith and kin, and not so very distantly related either, I have to be honest with you. The Kings of the Mountain have to be watched carefully at all times. You will do well to remember that. Even the weak ones need to be watched.'

'Yes,' Simon said, 'I think I know already.'

'Ah, no doubt. But now let me tell you about *her*. Came with a cauldron on her back she did, a great, black cauldron, and her shawl full of herbs and seedling plants—and a cutting from her vine.'

'*Her* vine!'

'Yes! This vine was hers, once upon a time, but I'll tell you of that later. She came wild and beautiful, the ideal wife for a mountain king, you would think—and my uncle did think so. Had she not been evil she would have been ideal, but he never found out about it till after he had married and lived with her a while. Folk never do find out such things except in such a fashion, and by then it is too late to save themselves, and so it was with him.

'She took his crown, took away his power, and then, Jones, then she brought forth darkness from that cauldron and spread it, scattered it, like some foul pestilence upon the mountain. And once sown, she nourished it with incantations and dancings and ritual offerings. I seen her once. In and out of the stones she went, to and fro, her feet not on the ground, I swear. Yes, I swear she never touched the ground.'

'In and out, between the Dancers of the Moon?' Simon asked.

'Yes, in and out among the Dancers. The crown gave her power over the Dancers, you see. That is what the crown is for—for controlling the power of the moon among the Dancers, *using* the power of the moon. The crown gave her mastery of the moon—at least, so I understand. O'Shaughnessy did say though, that she, with all her incantations, had not the power a crowned King would have with just one single song. Any road there she danced, among the stones, with the crown upon her head.'

'Golly! I can just see her, bathed in moonlight.' Fred was leaning forward, entranced by the picture Daniel had created.

'Ah no, Miss Fred, there was no moonlight. There

was never moonlight after *she* came. She drove away the moon, her and her darkness. And the moon had belonged in that place. No, that is not right! It was that place which belonged to the moon.'

'That's right,' Simon said. 'It was called the moon side of the mountain, wasn't it?'

'Indeed yes. It was moon, moon silver moon. Their whole life was governed by the moon—or was it that the moon was governed by their lives? I never understood. I was not born a King, you see. I was born cousin to the Kings. We cousins were never told exactly what went on, what was done, or what could be done. What they did with their crown and those stones in that circle was not for us to know. That was their secret. But my father did say that they could make those Dancers dance.'

'Brass bedknobs!' Fred sat back, upright suddenly. 'You mean they could make those tall stones get up and move?'

'Indeed yes, or so I heard,' Daniel said. 'They cannot do that now, of course, for the crown is gone—and that Amahiah wouldn't want to have anything to do with all that, any road, even if he had the crown.' It was obvious that Daniel didn't like his cousin Amahiah. 'I should be more tolerant of Amahiah, I know,' he said. 'Poor fellow, he had no name till he was seven and the school inspector got him to school and the Minister baptised him. No name! The disgrace of it! Neglected he was, and all alone up there, watching her carryings on day and night. No wonder it is that he turned against it all with such passion. You'll have to watch that Amahiah Jones. He will not want the crown found. He will stop you if he can. He will never want to see that crown again.'

'The crown, it's lost, then, and—and you said, you seem to think that I ought to be looking for it. B-but what I'm supposed to be doing is getting rid of the vine.' Simon was trying hard to see where he fitted in with this story of O'Shaughnessy, for he was sure that he must fit in with it somehow. He saw that Daniel was watching him carefully over the top of the flare of another match. 'Where do I fit in to all this?' he asked him. 'Fred said you specially wanted to talk to me, and you knew about the vine being there even though I hadn't told anyone about it, and I'm sure Dewi and Amahiah wouldn't have told anyone.'

'O'Shaughnessy told me about it,' Daniel said. 'All those years ago, he told me it would be there. He told me how it would come about, and he told me that when I heard of it, and of you, I was to tell you about him and about *her* and about the crown.'

'You mean he knew that Jonesy was going to be here now? But how could he know?' Fred was full of admiration for O'Shaughnessy. 'He must have been a marvellous wizard.'

'He was good . . . but not all that good,' Daniel said, and Simon saw that he was watching him again. 'He knew a thing or two more than *she* thought he did, though he was no match for her while she had the crown *and* the Cauldron, he said. It was because of the Cauldron that he came here, he said. It is an Irish cauldron, you see. *She* was in Ireland for a while, living and learning, and when she left she took the Cauldron with her although it was not hers. And O'Shaughnessy was sent to fetch it back.'

'Who sent him?' Simon asked.

'Now that he wouldn't tell me. But let me tell you what he *did* tell me. Let me tell you the message that he left for you. It happened like this . . .' Daniel settled down again.

'Just before O'Shaughnessy disappeared from the mountain, he came up here, to Tŷ Corn Du. Saw him come up the avenue, I did. I was working in the ha-ha, the very same one Miss Meryl is fussing about today. Well, saw him go striding by, I did, and he was singing his fighting song, and I thought to myself: "What's he up to?" and I downed tools and followed along after him. Into the house he went, as bold as brass, and next moment it was: "Stop thief! Help, help!" from Mrs Mathias who was housekeeper at the time, and out of the house comes

71

O'Shaughnessy again, and what has he stolen—the Black Horn.

'O-hoo!' Daniel chuckled. 'Now that was a fight we had then. That was a fight. Tried to swipe me with the Horn, he did, but I grabbed it and threw him, and he let go of it and I tossed it to Mrs Mathias. Then he laughed that great laugh of his, and we set to, and had a fight just for the fun of it. Loved a fight, did O'Shaughnessy, a good, clean—well *nearly* clean—fight. Naturally he got the better of me. I was no match for him, ever. And then I had to give him a song, as usual. Insisted on a song, he did, you see, from anyone he fought. Every fight had to end with a song.

'And then, when he'd had his song, "Danny boy," he said to me. Always called me Danny boy, he did. "Danny boy," he said, "it's a word with you I'm after having." And he put his great arm around my shoulders and steered me off with him right back to the ha-ha where I belonged. Knew I was there all the time, he did, the old rogue!

'Well, we shared my cake and cheese between us, and my water jug, and it seemed to me that the water had turned to wine, and my bara brith was like fine cake made with cream and honey. And he told me all I've told you about *her* and the Cauldron. And then he said: "Danny boy, she's going to finish me off. I've seen that it will be so. It's written on the wall

72

for me. She's going to finish me off with that devilish vine of hers, and it's not stopping her I'll be able. She's more than a match for me, with that Cauldron *and* the crown—but we'll have her yet, we will—me and him who's coming along this way shortly, him who'll be willing and able to use that Black Horn, that I was getting the feel of just now."

'He hadn't been trying to steal the Black Horn at all, see,' Daniel said. 'He'd just been seeing how it felt like so that he would be able to recognise it when he felt it again, he said, though what he meant exactly by that I do not know.

'Any road, he roared with laughter then, roared like I'd never heard him roar before. And "Danny boy," he said, "She'll be thinking that she's seen the last of me when she sends me off to die poisoned with that vine, but she'll be wrong there. She'll be more wrong than she's ever been in all her wicked life. There are ways and means of sending back that vine to her who gave it," he said, "and I know those ways and means. I'm going to send it back to her," he said. "Though I'm dead and gone for a hundred years I'll still send it back. Oh, she'll be sure to know about the cupful of little flowers," he said, "but that won't stop me. Send it back, I will till I'm after feeling the touch of that Black Horn again. Then I'll be knowing that the lad has come to finish the job that I've begun."

' "Lad?" I said, to him, and he said: "Yes, lad. Just a boy. That's on the wall too. Just a boy—and you, Danny, will still be here when he comes," he said to me. "You'll still be here, and you'll hear as to how that he's after asking about a strange vine that's up at the Castell, and what's it all about he'll be asking. And then you must step forward, Danny, and you must tell him every word of what I've been telling you this day. And you must tell him that *the crown is with me.* Don't tell that to another living soul. But tell it to him. And tell him to follow the vine to find me and the crown. And tell him, after that he has to get the King crowned again, and the two of them together can beat her and her dark army. The two of them together can give the moon back what is hers. Tell him that," he said.'

9. About the Vine and the Cauldron

There was so much to think about. Simon didn't even try to sleep. He lay in bed watching the moon racing the clouds above the carn. The moon, banished from her own place on the mountain, banished by a dark army.

Dark Army! That was what O'Shaughnessy had called the darkness—the Dark Army. And now, he and Dewi had to drive out that army and let the moon come back. He and Dewi Llewelyn. The thought made him despair. How on earth could he work with Dewi Llewelyn? It was impossible. Everything about this whole business was impossible, and working with Dewi was the most impossible of all. But he had to do it. He settled down to sort it all out in his mind, to get it all straight, to sort out what it was *exactly* that he had to do.

He had to give the far side of the mountain back to the moon. That was the ultimate aim, but to do that, first of all he would have to get rid of the darkness that had taken over the moon's side of the mountain. He knew what that darkness was now. That was one good thing! He knew that it was the Dark Army which Mamgu Llewelyn had brought out of the black Cauldron which stood in the scullery at the Castell. The way to get rid of the army was to work with the King of the Mountain and drive it away somehow. The King of the Mountain was going to have to be Dewi, not Amahiah, because Amahiah would never be interested in being King. So first he had to get Dewi crowned King, and that meant finding O'Shaughnessy, because O'Shaughnessy had the crown.

'Only he's dead, and that means he's going to look awful. He'll be a skeleton.' Simon began to dread finding O'Shaughnessy. 'Too bad!' he told himself. 'That's just too bad! A skeleton is only a skeleton, even if it's O'Shaughnessy's skeleton. Or is it! Will it be different? Will there be something not quite ordinary about it? It'll have the vine growing out of it, I suppose, so it won't be absolutely ordinary. And I still ought to get rid of that vine for Mrs Llewelyn. Without hurting O'Shaughnessy, of course.' He wondered if that would be possible. He would just have to hope so. But how would he get rid of the vine? There was always the cupful of little flowers that Mamgu had used, if he could only find out about it, but now that he knew a bit more about her, he didn't really want to do anything that Mamgu had done. So, how was he going to get rid of the vine? He worried about it for a while, then he thought: 'I wonder if *The Historian* can tell me how to do it!' he decided to look up 'vine'. He would have to be quiet. His mother had threatened all manner of retribution if he did just one more thing about what she called 'this Llewelyn business' that night. But he would risk it. He fetched his glasses and *The Historian,* and switched on the light.

He had to think very carefully before he found the right vine. He had to imagine how it looked, remember the blood dripping from it as it crept back into the walls of Castell Llewelyn, and think of every single detail Daniel had been able to tell him about it, before the pages of the book finally lay open and still. Then he read:

'*There is, in the WeSt Land, a certainne vine which wivves learned in wickedde arte do be able to use in the manufacture of poiSonne. This Same poiSonne they do form into a pellette which, by virtue of their powere they do affix beneath the teethe of their poore victimme, and there it do Staye til it do be removedde by the wivve who did affix it or elSe by one with greater power of honde than the wivve do have.*

If itt be not removvedded Surely it do growe again and Send forthe with vigour Sundry tendrilles and branches which do bleede copiouSly with the bloode of the poore victimme, and, verily, it do alSo be poSSESSed with the witte of the victimme and do grow whereSoever the victimme fo deSire it to growe.

This growethe may be checkedde with placing certainne Small bloSSommes upon the place wherein the poore victimme do be hidde. But theSe do check it only momentarily and muSt of neceSsity be renewedde at times til whenSoever the pellette may be removvedde and the vine therfore deStroyed for all time.

Simon stopped reading for a moment. This was marvellous! This was exactly what he needed to know, and, apart from the fact that he was going to have to put his hand into O'Shaughnessy's skeleton's mouth to take out the pellet of poison vine, he was very pleased with it all, for it meant that he would be able to find the crown and get rid of the vine for Mrs Llewelyn all at the same time.

But, first, he had to find O'Shaughnessy, and that might take a long time. 'O'Shaughnessy said I had to follow the vine,' he thought, 'But there's masses and masses of it. It's all through the walls up there.' He wondered how ever he could follow it through the walls, and whether Amahiah would let him, anyway. But then he realized that there might be an easier way of finding where the vine began. *The Historian* had said that the flowers had to be placed where the victim was hidden, so if he could only find out exactly where Mamgu had put her cupful of little flowers he would know exactly where O'Shaughnessy was. 'But will *they* know where she put it?' he wondered. 'And if they do will they tell me? Probably not,' he thought, 'but I'll give it a try. At least I'll have Fred there with me when I ask.'

Daniel had planned that. He had been quite adamant that Simon ought to have Fred with him when he went to find O'Shaughnessy. 'It's only fair that if he *can* have company he *ought* to have company,' he had said as they sat in the summer house talking about what O'Shaughnessy had said, and what Simon had to do. 'You ought to keep him company, Miss Fred,' he had said, 'that's what friends are for, for keeping company in nasty moments.' So Fred had said that she would come with him. She wasn't very happy about the idea. Nor was Simon, and, as usual, he felt very guilty about it. He told himself that it would be nice to have her with him. Hadn't he wanted her to come before? But her enthusiasm did worry him. And she *mustn't* begin to nag! And if she came with him when Dewi was there too he knew that there was no hope that he would be able to cope with both of them at once. 'But Fred only means to be helpful,' he told himself, 'and she *is* the best friend I've ever had. And it *will* be nice if she comes.'

He began to read again. *The Historian* actually gave a list of the flowers which were needed for the spell. 'Thyme, marjoram, chamomile, eyebright, dogs-mercury, tormentil and agrimony,' he read. He would remember their names. And how many of them were needed. 'Three of each kind. Twenty-one little flowers altogether.' Now he knew one of Mamgu's precious spells. '*So there. Dewi Llewelyn!*' he thought.

After that he looked up the Cauldron. 'Cauldron,' he thought, and he imagined it. He pictured it as he had seen it, in the shadows in the corner of the scullery at Castell Llewelyn. He remembered the dreadful feeling of darkness in and around it, and he thought about Ireland, and that O'Shaughnessy had said that the darkness was an Army . . . The pages

79

slid through his fingers, and when they lay still, again he read:

'There is in Erin a cauldron Similar to thatte ycleppte Ye Cauldron of Life, which being the gift of gretne Bran to the huSband of his SiSter Rhiannon. TheSe cauldrones in ye oldenne days did makke ye daed to live again. Whool armies on being Slaine were putte therin and did come oot not as corpSes but as livinge, fightinge men.'

Simon thought of the darkness. There was nothing living about the Dark Army over on the other side of the mountain, and it wasn't an army, either. 'It's just a . . . a presence or something,' he thought. 'It's not real and it's not alive. So why not? What's gone wrong with the Cauldron?'

He hoped that *The Historian* would explain, and, in a way, it did. It didn't give him facts about what had gone wrong with the Cauldron, but it did give him the opinion of the writer about what could easily go wrong with it.

'I do greatly feare,' the writer commented, *'Thatte this foul busineSSe of making ye daed to live againne do be bounde to comme to greif ere long. Verily itte do be So open to muddle and malpractice thatte Somme wickedde foole will Surely Some day bring forth, not living men, but Spirits and the darkneSs of deathe, and much evil will enSue.'*

'And he was right about that, all right,' Simon

thought, as he came to the end of the passage and rested the book on his knees again. 'Somewhere, at some time since he wrote that, someone either didn't know how to do it properly, or else deliberately did it wickedly and wrong. It might even have been Mamgu Llewelyn herself who did it. And now we have an army of spirits and darkness come out of the Cauldron . . . And how ever do I get rid of that? Do I put it back in the Cauldron? Do I send it away? I *still* don't know what exactly I have to do. And I've still got to get Dewi Llewelyn to co-operate.'

It was impossible. He would never do it. He put down *The Historian* and stood the Black Horn in its place beside his bed, and crept back beneath his quilt, and lay there feeling frightened and worried and hopeless, until, at last, he fell asleep.

10. O'Shaughnessy's Hiding Place

Simon nearly missed the school bus next morning. So did Dewi.

'Jones,' Dewi said, falling into a seat beside him as the bus moved off. 'Jones, I hope very much that you've overslept on account of staying up late to find out how to do this little job I've given you, because I, Jones, *I* overslept on account of you haven't done it yet.'

'That is the reason,' Simon said. 'I stayed up and found out quite a lot about it all last night.'

Dewi turned his head and stared at him critically. 'And pretty miserable it's made you too, by the look of you,' he said. 'What did you find out? That you *are* going to have to blast away with that old horn after all?'

'No.' Simon didn't want to talk to him. He didn't want to tell him anything, but he knew that he would have to, or he would have no peace all day. 'Actually, I found out all about the cupful of little flowers,' he said, and was amazed at himself, because he knew that he had chosen to say that especially to irritate Dewi.

'You don't say!' Dewi was irritated. 'What a clever little chap you are,' he said. 'And now you want to come up to my place and put your new-found knowledge into action. Is that it?'

'Yes,' Simon said, 'that's it.'

'Well,' Dewi sighed, 'I suppose I should say thank heavens for that, and look forward to a good night's sleep. There is one snag, however, Jones.'

'What's that?'

'Da's dead against you having anything whatsoever to do with those flowers, and with Da dead against it you'll be an idiot to try it.'

Now it was Simon's turn to sigh, but his sigh was genuine. 'I was hoping he'd be able to give me some information about them too,' he told him.

'I thought I heard you say you'd found out *all* about them,' Dewi said sarcastically.

'Yes, I did. I do. I know all their names and all th-that, b-but I don't know where to put them.'

Simon began to wish he hadn't mentioned the flowers as Dewi laughed rudely. 'Well, if you go anywhere near Da he'll tell you where to put them all right,' he said, 'and it will be very impolite of him too. No, you'd be better off coming over with that old horn and blasting the wretched thing, like I said.'

'That's not possible,' Simon told him coldly. 'Certainly I'll bring the Horn when I come over, but I won't be using it like that.'

'How will you be using it, then?' Dewi sounded genuinely interested as he asked this question, but Simon wouldn't tell him any more.

'It's none of your business,' he said.

'But it *is* my business, I think Jones,' Dewi said, 'and I think sooner or later you're going to have to appreciate that.'

'He never spoke a truer word,' Simon thought gloomily. 'Damn him! Damn him! Why does it have to be *him* that I've got to work with!'

Fred said almost the same thing that Dewi had said to him when she met him after school. 'Have you told that Llewelyn boy about this crown business yet?' she asked first, and when Simon told her that he hadn't, she said: 'Well, you'd better get a move on then, hadn't you. Brass bedknobs, he's got to know, Jonesy.'

'I know he has.' Simon trudged wearily along the lane beside Gwenhwyfar. 'But first I want to find it. I want to get all that part over and *then* tell him.'

'You're putting it off,' she said accusingly.

'Yes, putting it off until I've got over seeing O'Shaughnessy.'

'Oh, is that it! You're thinking of what O'Shaughnessy's going to be like. Well, he's only going to be a skeleton, Jonesy. Brass bedknobs, we've got one hanging in the bugs cupboard at school. They're nothing to be afraid of. Are they?'

Simon looked up at her. She didn't really believe everything she was saying. She was really as scared as he was. 'You don't have to come with me, you know,' he told her.

'Yes I do,' Fred said stubbornly. 'I've said I will, and I will, I must say I do wish you knew a bit more about what to *do* though.'

'Well, I do know a lot more than I did when I saw you last night, ' Simon said.

'Brass bedknobs! Why didn't you tell me!'

Fred looked a little less apprehensive about it all as he told her about the vine. But what he had to say about the Cauldron made her worry again. 'I hate cauldrons,' she said. 'I hate them. When I planned to be a witch myself. You know, before I met you. I always said I would never, ever have a cauldron. I hate them.'

What she really meant was that she was frightened of them. Simon understood that. He didn't blame her. 'You needn't come for that bit,' he said. 'I'll have told Dewi all about it by the time I get to that bit. I'll have his company then.'

'And that'll be all the more reason for having me there too, I should think,' Fred said. 'Let's get it over quickly, Jonesy.'

They arranged to meet right after breakfast next morning. Then Fred went home to help Miriam build a model of Totnes Station in the attic of Tŷ Corn Du, and Simon went home to worry about Dewi even more.

There had been trouble in school for Dewi that day. He had been asked by the headmaster to sing in assembly, and he had refused. He hadn't said: 'I'm sorry, I can't sing.' He had said: 'No, I won't sing,' and not even the headmaster with all his authority and fury could make him.

'And if he can't make him do what he doesn't want to do, how on earth am I going to make him?' Simon thought.

Fred arrived at Simon's house before breakfast next morning, and they ate toast and marmalade together in his kitchen, with his mother hovering, longing to ask what they were going to do, but not being brave enough to hear the answer. She contented herself with 'Be careful', as they went out.

Fred left Gwenhwyfar with Simon's mother. Bedwyr had been left with Guy. She was afraid that Brenin would fight him, and no doubt he would have, for he came rushing out at them, barking and circling furiously, as they walked along the last part of the Castell Llewelyn lane beside the Dancers of the Moon.

'It's just as well you're coming openly,' Fred said. 'You'd never have managed a quiet sneaky look around for O'Shaughnessy with *him* here, that's certain.'

'It would have been impossible even without him,' Simon said. 'Flippin' Amahiah never misses anything, nor does bloody Dewi.'

'Jonesy!' Fred looked at him with admiration. 'You sound quite fierce.'

'No I don't,' Simon said. 'I just sound fed-up with the bossy, big-headed lot of them.' He peered around. 'Can you see them anywhere?' he asked. 'I would have thought that one of them at least would have come out by now.'

'Amahiah's miles away on the other side of the

moor,' Fred said. 'At least, I suppose that must be him. There's no sign of Dewi. The horses are all in a field over there, but he's not there with them.'

'Good! Perhaps—' Simon looked around at the upright stones, standing tall and grey beside the path, 'perhaps I could just have a quick look at *them* first—before any one comes.'

'No chance!' Fred said. 'We've been seen.' Mrs Llewelyn had seen them. She was leaning from a bedroom window beckoning to them. 'We'd better see what she wants,' Fred said.

Mrs Llewelyn called quietly to them to come around to the back door, and when they met her there she put her finger to her lips. 'Dewi's sleeping still,' she said. 'Poor lamb, he's so tired. And you've brought Frederika with you, too. What a shame if he misses you. Perhaps you'll come in and wait a while?'

'Well, I think perhaps we'd better not wait. I think perhaps I ought to get on.' Simon began to hope that, maybe, with just a little luck, he might be able to look around without Dewi watching him and asking awkward questions.

Mrs. Llewelyn looked at him seriously. 'Dewi told me about you intending to use the cupful of little flowers,' she said. 'And you know all about them, too. There's wonderful!'

Simon was embarrassed. 'Well, actually, no. Actually I only know their names. I don't know how to use them. You know, I don't know where they have to be put.'

'But I can tell you that,' Mrs Llewelyn said. 'Mamgu always used to put them in the stone they call the First Dancer, the one that's over there, nearest the carn, the one all covered with the yellow, mossy stuff.'

'Oh, Mrs Llewelyn!' Fred was ecstatic. 'It's *you* who's wonderful. Now we can get on with it right away.'

'But you haven't got fresh flowers. Mamgu always—'

'Well, actually Jonesy doesn't need the flowers,' Fred told her confidentially. 'All he needs is the Black Horn. We'll just get on with it. Thank you ever so much. Come on, Jonesy,' she said. She gave Simon a push, and then steered him away quickly, towards the stone. 'Come on!' she said. 'Come on, before she starts to think she ought to let that wretched boy know what's going on. Come on!'

'You're rushing me,' Simon said.

'You need rushing.'

'No I don't. I need to be careful. And if you rush me when we're inside that circle—'

'Don't worry. I'm not coming inside the circle. I'm going to say outside. As a matter of fact not all those wild horses in that field over there would get me inside. But come on, now. Let's run!'

Simon ran after Fred across the wiry grass towards the edge of the stone circle. There Fred stopped. She shoved her hands in her pockets and hunched her shoulders against the cold wind and said: 'OK! In you go, Jonesy. I'll be right here—but I will come in if your shout for me.'

'Thanks,' Simon said, 'but I'll be all right. I won't shout. But if you see Amahiah coming, *you* shout, please.' He was more worried about Amahiah than he was about going into the stone cirle, but he didn't tell Fred that. 'Right! Here I go!' he said, and, with

the Black Horn held firmly in his hand, he stepped in among the Dancers of the Moon.

He felt their power at once. There was a tingling in his fingers and trembling somewhere in the pit of his stomach. He wasn't frightened. This wasn't terrible. This was exciting. He was in the presence of some great and ancient power, harnessed long, long ago, by this circle of stones. 'And the Llewelyns, with their crown, could *use* this power', he thought, and stood still, marvelling at it all. 'No wonder they're Kings of the Mountain, with all this power! And Dewi,' he thought, 'Dewi Llewelyn will have all this power when he's been crowned King.' The thought was worrying. Dewi, the conceited, headstrong Dewi, with all this power. It didn't seem sensible. 'But Daniel says the Kings of the Mountain are always like Dewi, so it must be all right. I'll just have to hope he doesn't decide to do anything with it that he's not supposed to do. But it's no good worrying about that. I must get on with this.'

He began to look around carefully. He found the flowers that Mamgu had left there. They were exactly where Mrs Llewelyn had said they would be, in a cup-shaped hollow, carved into the lichen-covered stone, on the side which faced into the circle.

He could see why Mamgu's spell had stopped working. The flowers were no longer like flowers.

90

They were dry and brown and fragile, nothing but brown dust, stuck together by last summer's sunshine. Simon crumbled them between his fingers and then tossed them up into the wind that blew towards the carn. It caught them, and whisked them away, sparkling suddenly, caught in one beam of sunshine. Now that spell was lost and gone for ever.

And now he must find O'Shaughnessy. 'She had to put the flowers on the place where he was hiding from her, so he must be right here.' Simon looked at the stone carefully. He walked around it once or twice. There was no sign of the vine there at all, but O'Shaughnessy had to be there. This had to be the place. Simon began to look for a grave. Then he realised that that was silly. If O'Shaughnessy had been in a grave, Mamgu would have been able to dig him up and take the pellet from his mouth and stop the vine permanently. And anyway, he wouldn't have been able to bury himself. No, the idea of a grave was ridiculous. So, where was he?

There was only one place where he could be. 'He's underneath this stone. Yes! Of course he is! Somehow, he managed to hide away from her underneath this stone, and she couldn't get at him because she needed the crown to help her move the stone out of the way and he's got the crown underneath it with him. Brilliant! He was brilliant . . .! But how do *I* move the stone? Oh, with my hands and the Black Horn, of course. And the moment I use the Black Horn O'Shaughnessy will know I'm here because he managed to find out what it felt like before she killed him. He thought of everything. Right, O'Shaughnessy, let's let you know that it's all going according to plan—so far.'

He stood still for a moment not knowing what exactly to do. Suddenly he felt surrounded, trapped by the stones, the giant stones, giant dancers. For a moment he was frightened. Quickly, he glanced up at the carn for reassurrance, *his* carn, no matter what Dewi Llewelyn said. And then he noticed something.

He noticed that the first Dancer of the Moon stood directly in line with the carn, and, with the Black Horn in his hands, the tall, grey stone seemed actually to be one of the grey stones of the carn. It was as if the distance between them had vanished. The first Dancer was part of the carn. It even had the same yellow lichen growing on its side.

'It's a carn stone. It's all right for me to use it. I'll be quite safe with that stone, no matter what I do.' Confidently, Simon stepped towards the stone. 'Now! The Horn! Now!' He reached out, and touched the first Dancer very gently with the extreme tip of the Black Horn.

There was a shiver, a tingling in the air. The stone trembled. And the ground around his feet shook.

Then came stillness. The movement was not frightening. The stillness was. If it had lasted longer than one brief moment, Simon would have been terrified. He had upset the balance of the stones. He had disturbed their equilibrium. It was all right. It wasn't permanent. The circle was safe again. But it had been more dangerous than he thought it would be. 'O'Shaughnessy *must* have felt that,' Simon thought.

He stood still, listening and watching and feeling with his mind. Would there be some sign to tell him that O'Shaughnessy had felt the touch of the Horn and knew that he was there? Would there be some sign?

There was. A sigh came to him, long and low, like the sound of the wind from the west, soughing through pine trees, A sigh, seeping, welling up from deep beneath the first Dancer of the Moon.

The sigh faded and went. Simon stood still again. That couldn't be all. There would be more. Something else was going to happen. He could feel it. Something was coming—something. He stood waiting—waiting and watching . . . And, at last, he saw the sign that he was looking for.

It was just one, fragile, wisping tendril of the vine, the growing tip, that had struggled through darkness towards light. And it was growing out from beneath the foot of the first Dancer of the Moon. He watched it wisping, curling. It waved a tendril. It reminded him of a sea anemone, searching, feeling. It was fascinating. He stepped nearer. 'He's checking up. He's not sure if he dares to believe what he felt. He's thinking: "Was that or was that not the Black Horn?". I'd better let him know that it was.'

He stepped closer to the searching tendril, and reached out and touched it carefully with the Horn.

For a moment the tendril seemed to hang, suspended by some invisible thread. Then, carefully, it too reached forward, and it touched the Black Horn, just once, one cautious, feeling touch. Then it sank, limply, to the ground.

Simon watched it then as it retreated, writhing, back into the earth from where it has grown, back beneath the first Dancer of the Moon.

'And that's where I've got to find O'Shaughnessy and the crown.' Simon felt excited. He would go down there now. He would have to move the stone, but that would be all right. It would be safe, for a while. He would move it with his hands. One hand holding the Horn, the other pushing the stone. He had done that sort of thing before. He would do it now, quickly. He reached out . . .

And then Fred called. 'Simon—Amahiah's coming!'

Simon looked back at her across the stone circle.

She was pointing, urgently, towards the moor. But he didn't look where she was pointing. He looked past her, at Castell Llewelyn, at a window, Dewi's window. There, he could see, quite clearly, because of the Black Horn in his hand, Dewi standing, watching him . . . And he knew that Dewi had seen everything that had happened.

11. The Problem of Dewi

They could only stand and wait. It was no good running. Fred wanted to. She was just as scared of Amahiah as Simon was. But Simon wouldn't run. 'He'll only chase us and catch us,' he said, but that wasn't the real reason why he had to stand there and wait while Amahiah trundled towards them on his tractor. The real reason was that he wasn't going to run away while Dewi was watching. He wasn't going to give Dewi one single opportunity to sneer and jeer at him because he was afraid. That was important. Dewi must never ever know when he was afraid.

'And he saw the vine. He saw it all. He saw what I did!' That was far more worrying than Amahiah's rapidly approaching rage and wrath. With one, last, careful look at Dewi in his window, Simon turned to wait for Amahiah.

But then Fred said, 'Mrs Llewelyn's coming!' And Mrs Llewelyn saved them. 'The vine ... it's vanished! It's gone!' she told Amahiah joyfully. 'He's got rid of it, and without using the cupful of flowers, too. He did as you said. He never stirred up all Mamgu's old carryings-on again after all. So there's nothing for you to be annoyed about,' she said.

Amahiah glared. He opened his mouth as though he was going to say something angrily, but then he shut his mouth again in a grim, tight line. He glanced distastefully at the Black Horn, and then stood for a moment looking out of the corners of his eyes at the Dancers of the Moon. His head was slightly tilted to one side, as though he was listening, apprehensively, for something. But nothing, no noise, came, and he climbed back on his tractor again and roared away, leaving Mrs Llewelyn to say thank you.

'What was all that about?' Fred asked as they began to walk back across the moor.

'I did do something he didn't want me to do.' Simon explained. 'I went into the circle. I don't think he was too bothered about the actual cupful of flowers. It was the fact that I would have to go into the circle to use them that he didn't like. It's the Dancers of the Moon that he wants left alone for ever and ever. *He* doesn't want to be King of the Mountain, and he doesn't want Dewi to be King either. I wonder if he saw Dewi watching me . . .'

'Was he watching you? I didn't see him. And how could *you* have?' Fred was still very worried about it all, and when Simon explained about being able to see Dewi when he had the Horn in his hands, she looked as though she was going to despair. 'You're going to have to bring him in on it, Simon,' she said. 'He's a special part of it all. You know he is. You can't do it without him.'

'I want to find the crown first.' Simon was determined to keep to his plan . . . but he did wish that Fred would call him Jonesy and start 'brass bedknobbing' again. He didn't like it when Fred was too worried to 'brass bedknob'.

They trudged along in silence until they reached the carn, then they stopped so that Simon could look at the Islands and describe them to Fred. They changed, those Islands. They seemed different every time he looked at them. Today they rose mysteriously through light sea mist, so close, somehow, that it was as though the veil of mist had given them confidence to creep nearer the mountain. He saluted them with the Black Horn, and a window, high in the tower beneath the red banner, flashed gold. It was like a signal, acknowledging the salute. He had seen it do that before. He didn't think it was a coincidence. Just as *he* watched the Islands, so someone there watched the mountain. Someone was watching, always.

On the way down the mountain, Fred began to talk about Dewi again. 'You're going to need him to help you find the crown,' she said. 'You're going to have to get him to invite you to tea again, or something, or you'll never get back to Castell Llewelyn. There's no way you're going to sneak up, even at night. The dog will bark. You're going to have to tell Dewi and get him to invite you back.'

'No! There must be another way. I'll think of another way,' Simon said, but it was Daniel who thought of another way. Fred told him all about their morning, and the problem of Dewi, and then phoned Simon to tell him that Daniel had suggested a solution.

'Jonesy! Daniel's come up with a fabulous idea . . . Go tomorrow! It's Sunday. The Llewelyns are Chapel. They go *three* times. You—*we* will have all day . . .!'

Fred arrived in time for breakfast again next morning, and they set out feeling reasonably hopeful and optimistic, though Simon did feel that it was suddenly all too easy. Something would go wrong, he thought.

It did. When they reached the carn, Dewi was

waiting for them there. He was sitting astride his pony with the rest of the herd behind him. He blocked the path. He knew he was blocking it, but he didn't get down from his pony, nor did he move the herd out of the way. He just sat there, and watched them coming.

'Oh lor!' Fred stopped and waited for Simon to catch up with her. 'It's *him*! He stayed home from Chapel. He must have guessed. Oh lor!' she said.

'Don't stop! Don't let him see you're bothered. Just keep on walking.' Simon pushed past her and led the way. He hoped, very much, that he looked more brave than he felt. He walked as close to Dewi as he dared, then he stood still and looked at him. At first, neither of them said anything. Then Dewi spoke. 'Going somewhere, Jones!' he asked, casually and arrogantly.

'You're going to have to—you know, like I said.' Fred began, in a rush, before Simon could answer.

'You keep out of this, Miss Tŷ Corn Du,' Dewi told her coldly. 'This is between me and him.'

'Simon!' Fred was upset and about to panic.

'All right!' Simon said, trying not to sound frantic. 'All right, I'll tell him everything now.'

The look in Dewi's eyes was nasty. 'That's very *nice* of you, I'm sure,' he said to Simon. 'Most kind . . . but let's see if I can teach you a thing or two first, shall we.'

'All right,' Simon said. He was beginning to feel rather scared. The horses were stamping restlessly. They surged forward. They tossed their heads. He almost stepped back . . . but he didn't. He managed to stand still. Holding the Black Horn in both hands across his chest, he stood and faced up to Dewi.

And now Dewi was looking at the Black Horn, looking at the Horn, looking at Simon's face, then back at the Horn. Then he looked past Simon at the Islands, and, suddenly, the anger drained from his face and he looked down at Simon with that dreadful, blank look which showed nothing and yet everything about the way he was feeling. 'You're up to something, Jones Corn Du, I know you are. I seen you yesterday, among the Dancers. Up to something you were, and you still are— and Da knows you are, only he won't admit it. Da's like a—like a—I don't know what he's like. But he knows there's more to all this than one old vine. He knows there's more to happen yet. He knows, but he won't tell me about it, and he should tell me. I know he should, because it's all to do with me. I *feel* it is, but I don't *know*.'

He slid from the pony's back. 'Let's talk sensible about this, Jones,' he said. 'I want to talk sensible. I want somebody to talk sensible to me. Da won't. So it's got to be you.'

Once again they were sitting on the carn looking at the Islands and talking. Dewi didn't like Fred being there, but Fred kept quiet and just listened and let him ignore her.

'All this is something to do with me being King of the Mountain. I can feel it is,' Dewi said. 'I felt it when I seen you there, in among the Dancers. I felt I should be in there too. I thought: how is it that this incomer from Petts Wood, can go in among *my* stones and I, who am born here, *can't* go in among them? And I felt that I *could*. I felt that I *should*. I *felt* it. Only I'm too terrified of them to do it.' He swore his long oath in Welsh. 'Duw, I'm so terrified of them! And I hate myself for being terrified, and you so cool and . . . and in control.' He frowned at Simon. 'How is it you're not terrified of them, Jones?' he demanded.

'Because the Dancers are nothing to be terrified of. Well, most of the time, they're not.' Simon tried to explain to him. 'You have to be careful when you're in among them. You have to be sensible what you do.'

'Yeh, yeh, but, given that, they're OK, are they?' Dewi grinned slyly. 'Or are they better than OK?' he looked out at the Islands. 'Are they like them? Are they marvellous?'

Simon didn't know what to say. He wanted to be honest with Dewi, but he didn't want to encourage him too much. In fact, the last thing in the world that he wanted to do that morning was encourage him. 'What makes you think they're like that?' he asked, still being careful.

'Because last night Da talked about them the same way he talks about the Islands. "Avert thine eyes," and all that guff.' He shook his head at Simon. 'We had a right day of it yesterday, Jones bach, me and Mam, because of you.'

'He got cross, did he?' Simon said.

'Cross! Jones, a King of the Mountain, even one like my Da, doesn't get cross. He rages. And that's what Da did, especially when he found out Mam had told you the place where it was all done.' He laughed. 'They had a right old row. Never seen Mam answer back like that, I hadn't.' He watched Simon now as he spoke. 'The funny thing was, it turned from being a row about *you*, to being a row about *Mamgu.*'

'What did they say about Mamgu?' Simon knew that Dewi was watching him. He was more careful than ever.

'Not a lot,' Dewi said, 'but there was another funny thing there too.'

'What was that?'

'They both hated dear old Mamgu,' Dewi said. 'Now why was that, Jones, I wonder?'

'I couldn't say.'

'Jones, don't treat me like an idiot,' Dewi said wearily.

And then Fred joined in. 'No, Jonesy,' she said, 'don't treat him like an idiot. He's got to know all about her.'

She was going to nag. She was beginning to interfere. 'Fred, don't . . .' he began.

But Fred went on. 'I know what's the matter with you', she said. 'You're afraid to tell him the truth about his grandmother in case it upsets him or hurts his feelings. Well, for goodness sake! He hasn't got any feelings to hurt.'

'He has!'

'Well, too bad. He's got to know about her.' She whirled round to face Dewi. 'Listen!' she said. 'There are times when you have to listen to things about people that you don't want to listen to. *I* had to when my mother went off. I didn't like it, and you're not going to like this, but you've got to know it because Simon can't explain anything to you unless you know this first. Your mamgu was a very nasty old woman—a very *wicked* old woman, to be quite accurate. It was her who made your side of the mountain so terrible and dark, and it was her who deliberately made you terrified of your Dancers so that you wouldn't find out how to be a *real* King of the Mountain.'

Dewi's face was expressionless again. He stared at Simon. 'Is that true?' he asked. Simon nodded, and

Dewi looked away from him and stared over his head at the Islands.

Simon watched him. What would he do? Would he get angry? Would he start throwing things? Would he do something nasty?

All Dewi did was shrug his shoulders and sigh. 'Well, to be quite honest with you I'd been thinking that she might be that way inclined,' he said. 'Just lately, one or two things I heard . . . OK, Jones, let me have it. What did she tell me that she shouldn't have and what didn't she tell me that she should?'

Simon told Dewi the story that Daniel had told him. He told him all about Mamgu, and the Cauldron, and the Dark Army, and O'Shaughnessy—and about the crown.

And it was about the crown that Dewi was most interested. 'A crown, eh!' His eyes sparkled. 'So I should have a crown. Ha! A Crown!'

'Yes,' Simon said carefully. He was beginning to feel worried. 'Yes, there is a crown, but you must be careful about wearing it.'

Dewi grinned at him. 'Don't you want me to wear it? Is that it? Jealous are you because now you're not the only one with something special?'

'Of all the—!' Fred almost exploded with exasperation. 'You're insufferable. You great twit!' she told him furiously. 'Of course he's not jealous.

Why ever should he be? The Black Horn's better than any old crown any day.'

'Is it indeed?' Dewi laughed at her. 'We'll see about that,' he said. And then he became extremely businesslike. 'Right, Jones, if we're going to get my crown back from old O'Shaughnessy, we'd better get a move on. Chapel doesn't last for ever, it only seems like that. Now!' He stood up and looked down at Simon. 'Now, if you want me to come and do this with you, Jones, you're going to have to leave *her* behind.' He jerked his thumb at Fred. 'And that's an ultimatum. I mean it.'

Simon stood up too. Dewi towering over him was making him feel dominated. He didn't like it. But he did like the idea of leaving Fred behind, though, as always, he felt guilty about it. 'But she didn't want to come,' he told himself, 'and she'll be safer if she doesn't come.' The problem was, how was he going to agree with Dewi without making Fred feel that he was letting her down, and without making Dewi feel that he was giving in to him?

He dealt with Dewi first. 'If I want Fred to stay, she stays, as long as she wants to,' he told Dewi. Then he turned to Fred. 'But I do think it might be a good idea, this time, if you didn't come with me,' he said to her. Fred shook her head. She looked as though she was going to cry. 'I'll be all right,' he said. 'I won't be on my own.'

'I know that, but it doesn't make it any better for you, does it.' Fred glanced at Dewi. 'He's not the sort of company I'd chose.'

'I haven't exactly chosen him either, have I?' Simon said. Behind him he heard Dewi mutter: 'Nice to be welcome,' but he ignored him. Dewi didn't care whether he was welcome or not. He wasn't upset, but Fred was. 'Listen,' he said to her. 'I think you would be much more use if you stayed behind. For one thing I'll only have myself to look after if—if anything goes wrong. It's dangerous, all this Dancers business, you know, or it could be anyway. And I don't know a lot about O'Shaughnessy either, do I? So I really think it would be better if you stayed up here out of it all but where you can still see what's going on.'

'So that I can get help if you need it,' Fred liked that idea. 'But who could I ask to help?'

'My Da,' Dewi said and sniggered when he saw her look horrified.

'No, not his father,' Simon told her. 'Go to Daniel. He'd think of something to do.'

'Yes—yes, he probably would, wouldn't he.' Fred made up her mind. 'All right. I'll stay here. No, I won't. I'll wait where I can see the Dancers, then I can watch what's happening.'

'Great!' Simon said. 'Thanks!'

Within minutes, Fred and Simon were walking

down across the moor to the small, grey crag which stood in the middle of the dark side of the mountain, half hiding the true crag from Castell Llewelyn. Dewi had galloped ahead to shut the horses in their field and be ready to go with Simon as soon as he arrived. They watched him galloping away from them, his long hair blowing behind him. 'King of the Mountain', Simon said.

'Yes, King of the Mountain, and as big-headed as any of them have ever been,' Fred said. 'You've got to watch him, Simon. Remember, Daniel said watch him.' She looked worried. 'Simon.' She was very serious. 'I know you don't like using The Black Horn as a weapon, but you might have to, you know.'

'Against Dewi, do you mean?'

'Yes. There's going to be no holding him, you know, when he get's his hands on that crown.'

'I'll have to persuade him to be sensible.'

'Oh come off it! You'll never do that. When he get's his hands on that crown, you're going to have to *make* him behave himself,' Fred said, and Simon knew that she was right. Before that day was over it would be the Black Horn against the crown of the Kings of the Mountain. It was not a fight which Simon was confident that he would win. Its outcome would depend entirely on the way he used the Black Horn.

12. Beneath the Dancer of the Moon

When Simon arrived at the Dancers of the Moon, the horses were shut safely in their high-walled field, and Dewi was standing waiting for him with a powerful torch in his hand.

'You never thought of bringing a torch, did you, Jones,' He flashed the beam in Simon's face. 'Good job you've got me with you or you'd be really in the dark,' he said.

The beam hurt Simon's eyes. In fact it half-blinded him for a moment, but he didn't let Dewi know, and he didn't say anything about the torch. He hadn't forgotten one. He simply hadn't brought one. He had remembered the blue light which had flowed from the cave where he and Fred had found the Unicorn. There would be light beneath this stone, too. He was sure of it. But he said nothing.

He glanced at Dewi as they stepped in to the stone circle. He thought he was still very frightened of the Dancers, but it was difficult to tell. He was pale, and he was looking at the stones sideways out of the corners of his eyes, in the way Amahiah had looked at them, and he didn't push in front as he usually did. In fact, he was moving very slowly.

'We'd better get a move on,' Simon said.

Dewi shook his head. 'Hang about first.' He caught hold of Simon's arm. 'First I want to know what to expect. What's going to happen? What, exactly, are you planning to do?'

'I'm going to move the first Dancer so that we can see what's under it.'

'*Move* the Dancer! You idiot!'

'I've got to move it,' Simon said. 'We can't get underneath it if I don't. We can't dig all around it, can we? Be sensible. It'll be all right, honestly. I'm sure it will.'

'Jones, I hope you *are* sure.' Dewi's voice was small and tight. 'OK, go on, move it—but for pity's sake be careful.'

Simon almost wanted to laugh. Fancy Dewi Llewelyn telling *him* to be careful! He walked right up to the first Dancer, just as he had done before. He tried to concentrate. It was difficult with Dewi so close that he could feel him brushing against his arm. The stone towered above him. He looked up at it, and for one moment he had a strange feeling that it knew what he was going to do to it. He hesitated. Could he do it? Was it safe? 'It'll be safe as long as I only use my hand,' he thought. 'Just my hand. I'd better not touch it with the Horn this time. No, I mustn't *move* it with the Horn.' He had a terrifying vision of all that power balanced so finely between these stones sent roaring askew and awry. No, he mustn't upset that power with the power of the Horn.

He reached out quickly, placing his left hand against the stone's grey side, just above the carved hollow where the cupful of little flowers had lain. Strangely, the stone was warm though the moor was icy cold. He gripped the Black Horn in his right hand, and then, very gently and carefully, he leant against the stone and pushed.

It was easy. Too easy perhaps? The first Dancer of the Moon slid aside with only the faintest graunch of stone against stone, and just the slightest tremble of earth beneath his feet.

Beneath the stone lay a trap-door. That, too, opened easily. And beneath that a steep, stone stairway led down, straight into the mountain.

Dewi peered past Simon. 'What is it? Steps? Let's have a look.' he flashed the torch. 'Duw, it's dark down there.'

'It isn't. At least, I don't think it is. Put out the torch a minute, and let's have a look.'

'Have a look at what?'

'At the light down there.' In spite of feeling frightened, Simon was excited. He had been right about there being a light—*almost* right—for this light wasn't blue, like the light around the Unicorn. This light was silver. 'It's silver, like moonlight,' he whispered. 'It's like moonlight—and this is the moon's side of the mountain.'

He looked at Dewi to see if he was excited too, but

Dewi wasn't even listening to him. He was flashing his torch again, along the walls of the stairway. 'Jones!' he hissed in a stage whisper. 'Look at these walls! Look at the work in them. Look at the fit of these stones. Duw, Da ought to see this. It's just like we build our walls still. It's us who built these, us Kings. For donkey's years we've been building stone walls *inside* our mountain as well as all over it. Aw, look at this!'

'Come on!' Simon wanted to make him hurry. 'We can't stay here looking at them now. Move down the stairs a bit more, then I can put the Dancer back in place.'

'No!' Dewi almost panicked when he heard that. 'No! You idiot! Don't do that. You'll have us trapped down here—all shut in, any road. I can't stand being shut in. And down here! Duw, no! Leave it open for pity's sake.'

Simon didn't like this. He ought to move the stone back into place. There was the balance of the circle to be considered. But he couldn't have Dewi panicking. 'All right,' he said, 'but we mustn't leave it like this too long. We must be quick.'

They hurried down the stairway. It ended in a short tunnel. That, too, was lined with stone walls. They walked along it together, and side by side, stepped out into the silver light.

It *was* moonlight. Simon knew it was. It was silver moonlight, shining from the walls of an enormous cave. They were moon-coloured walls, smooth and polished, and never made by human hands. Simon allowed himself one moment to thrill and marvel at those walls and the great power of magic which must have created them. Then he looked for O'Shaughnessy.

At first, he couldn't see him. At first the whole cave seemed to have nothing in it but moonlight and vine. It was filled with vine a great green network of it, twined and angled like creepers in a jungle. But O'Shaughnessy must be there too. He would be at the centre, at the root. That was where O'Shaughnessy would be. Simon took another step forward—and then he saw him.

O'Shaughnessy was a skull. 'Only a skull!' What had happened to the rest of him, Simon wondered. 'Only his skull.' This was important. It meant something. But he didn't know why it was important or what it meant. He stood still and looked at it.

The skull looked unpleasantly like a funnel-web spider, lying in wait at the end of the tube it had woven so skilfully to catch the unsuspecting fly.

'And who's the fly?' Simon thought. He could hear Dewi breathing heavily behind him.

'You can't go in *there*, Jones,' Dewi whispered. *'I'm* not going in.'

'We've got to go in,' Simon whispered back. He swallowed hard. He felt ill. *'I've* got to go in, anyway. I'll go first, and I'll try to get rid of the vine.'

'That's it. Blast it!'

'No! There's no need. All I've got to do is get the lozenge *she* gave him out of his mouth.'

'You can't do *that!* Blast him! Go on! Don't be an idiot.'

'I can't blast him—I won't. I'm going to get the lozenge out.' Simon stepped in to what he could now only think of as the mouth of the long, green tube. He half expected O'Shaughnessy to rush out at him, as the spider would have rushed out. He knew that O'Shaughnessy was going to do something. He could feel it. But what was he going to do, and, indeed, why should he do anything? They were supposed to be working together at this, weren't they? But O'Shaughnessy was going to do something.

Suddenly he knew what it was. 'He's going to start

a fight,' he thought. 'He loves a fight. He's going to start a fight.'

And that was exactly what O'Shaughnessy did. He waited until Simon was halfway along that long, green tube, then he dropped the vine. Instantly, Simon was caught by a twining, gripping stem which felt like a long, strong arm—the arm of an Irish wrestler. He felt O'Shaughnessy try to twist the Horn away from him, and held on to it as he had never held on to it before. Then he was lifted and spun and dumped on his back in a sea of green leaves. At the same time he heard Dewi shout, and knew that O'Shaughnessy was fighting him too.

Dewi shouted as though he was in terror of being torn apart. He had to tell him about O'Shaughnessy. He had to remind him of what Daniel had said about him. Somehow he had to shout, to explain what was going on.

He tried to stand up, but was thrown down again. He tried a second time. This time he was spun head-over-heels before being thrown. 'He's having fun,' he thought. How could he stop him? He mustn't hurt him. But this was ridiculous.

He had an idea. He would hold the Black Horn in both his hands, one hand at each end of it, so that he couldn't possibly make lightning with it. Then it would be safe to fight with it. He would push at the vine with it. He wouldn't hit it. He would push at it.

He rolled on to his side, twisted the Horn until he could grip near the pointed end with his left hand, while still holding the blunt end in his right. Then he pushed.

It worked. O'Shaughnessy pulled back as though he had been stung. Now Simon could stand up. Now he could shout. 'Dewi!' he called. 'Dewi!' He couldn't see him anywhere, but then he heard his voice somewhere beneath the vine on his left.

'The beggar's got me pinned down. He's got a grip on me. Blast him, Jones. Blast him!'

'No, no! Fight him. *You* fight him,' Simon shouted at Dewi. 'He wants a fight. That's all. He won't kill us. That's not his style. He just loves a fight. So fight! Give him a—' O'Shaughnessy gripped him and threw him again. He heard Dewi shout something at him in Welsh. He still sounded frightened. Had he listened? Would he take any notice? Simon waited, almost frantic. Dewi must join in, he must. With relief he heard him, suddenly. 'OK,' Dewi called to him. 'OK, Jones bach. If that's his game, he's on. Both together is it? Ready?'

'Ready!'

'Come on then!'

After that the fight was almost fun. Dewi seemed to enjoy it, anyway, and at the end, when at last O'Shaughnessy had stopped throwing them around Simon heard him laugh his wild shout of a laugh. He

115

stood up then, and peered across the cave. He could see that Dewi was standing up too, and looking across at him. They were some way apart, with the now even more tangled vine between them. Simon pushed his glasses back on properly. He saw that Dewi's shirt was torn, and he had a rip in his own sleeve, and what felt like a bruise coming up on the side of his jaw.

'Is that it?' Dewi was laughing. 'What's next?' he said. He sounded arrogant and very pleased with himself. Simon didn't like it.

'I'll get that lozenge out of his mouth.' Simon was trying to think. If he could keep doing things himself, it might stop Dewi doing something he shouldn't do. He tried to move towards the place where he thought he had seen O'Shaughnessy. He took one step and the vine tightened around his legs. He waited a moment, then tried again. Again the vine tightened. 'He won't let me move,' he said.

'What's he want—another fight?' Dewi laughed loudly.

'No, not a fight.' Simon thought of Daniel's story. 'He doesn't want another fight, It's a song he wants now—a song.'

As Simon said the words 'a song' it was as though another part of O'Shaughnessy's plan fitted into place. Had it been written on the wall for O'Shaughnessy that Dewi Llewelyn the King of the

Mountain *wouldn't* sing? It must have been. For now O'Shaughnessy had made a situation where Dewi, if he wanted his crown, was going to have to sing. 'Brilliant!' Simon thought.

'*You* have to sing to him,' he told Dewi. He watched Dewi's face, and knew that he was remembering the last time he had sung, to phantoms at Mamgu's funeral. That had been another part of Mamgu's cunning schemes to stop the Kings coming back into power. 'This is a trick,' Dewi said. 'It's a trick to make me do what I don't want to do.'

'It's to make you do what you've got to do,' Simon said. 'The Kings of the Mountain always have to sing. It's part of their power, somehow.'

'What do you know about it?' Dewi was angry.

'Just a bit more than you do,' Simon said. 'You've got to sing—or you don't get back your crown.'

Dewi was furious now. He swore in Welsh, and hit out at the vine. Then he snarled at Simon. 'What do I sing then?' he said. 'Go on, tell me, suggest something. What shall I sing?'

Simon thought frantically. What had he used to enjoy singing before all this horror stopped him singing? 'I know! Sing your rebel song,' he said.

'My rebel song?' Dewi didn't know what he meant.

'You know! The one that makes them furious at school,' Simon told him.

117

Then Dewi laughed again. 'My rebel song! Is that what you call it? Jones of the Black Horn from Petts Wood, I'll have you know that that ancient Welsh song is the song of the Kings of the Mountain,' he said proudly. And then he began to sing.

He began quietly, as though he still wasn't quite sure that he wanted to sing, but, soon, his voice came as sure and clear as it has always been, and music rose to fill the cave beneath the Dancers of the Moon.

As Simon listened to the song, now that he knew what it was, he could recognise some of the words. There was 'brenin' of course, and 'lleuad' which he knew meant 'moon', and one or two others, but most of the words he did not know, and he couldn't even guess what the song was saying.

There was, however, one thing he was absolutely sure of as he listened to it now, and that was that O'Shaughnessy was listening to it too. He could feel him listening, waiting for every word. It was a song that O'Shaughnessy knew. 'He must have heard Dewi's grandfather singing it. That's why he knew it. And he knows that it's special. Yes, it's special.' Simon began to walk towards O'Shaughnessy. He could do it now. The vine didn't stop him. He went very carefully, stepping over it, lifting it, gently, out of his way, He didn't want to disturb O'Shaughnessy as he listened to this special song of the Kings of the Mountain.

He reached him just as Dewi sang his last, few notes. The mouth of the skull grinned horribly. It was ugly. He wanted to close his eyes and not look at it. But he must look. He had to be careful. He mustn't fumble. He must get it right.

Quickly, he thrust his left hand into the terrible mouth. Only his fingers would fit. He felt around. Yes, there was the lozenge, there right behind the teeth, stuck tightly to the bone, exactly where *The Historian* had said it would be. He hooked his fingers around it. There was a short, sharp hiss—and the lozenge lay in his hand.

The effect was startling. Even as Simon straightened his back and stood up, the vine disappeared. There was another hiss, louder than the first and a puff of dust, and the vine was gone.

It was sudden and complete. The vine was gone. Quite gone. Where had it been? It *had* existed, hadn't it? If he hadn't fought with it, and still had bruises and a torn shirt to prove that he had fought with it, Simon knew that he would have been tempted to believe that the vine had all been one big illusion.

Dewi had no doubts about it whatsoever. 'We've beaten him. We've won!' He was jubilant. Simon was amazed at him. It was as though even the memory of the terror which had almost paralysed him had disappeared instantly as the vine disappeared. 'No, that's not it,' he thought. 'It wasn't then, that he stopped being frightened. It was while he sang. And, oh my goodness, just look at him now!'

He watched Dewi as he swaggered across the cave, and stood, triumphantly, over O'Shaughnessy. For one awful moment he thought he was going to kick the skull out of his way. He stepped forward. He couldn't let him do that. He must stop him.

But Dewi wasn't looking at O'Shaughnessy. He was looking behind him. He bent forward, arching over him, and reached out. 'Ah!' he said. 'Ah! Just see what we have here!' He laughed, and he stood up. He was holding the crown of the Kings of the Mountain.

The crown was beautiful. It was simple and exquisite. A plain, gold band held a crescent moon and a constellation of stars. The stars were diamonds, and the moon was pure silver. There were no other jewels, no scrolls, no surplus decoration, just the stars of diamonds and the moon of silver in stark simplicity.

Dewi's eyes were gleaming with triumph. 'My crown!' he said. '*My* crown!' And before Simon could even begin to try to stop him, he lifted the crown and set it firmly upon his head.

The gold band pressed Dewi's dark hair close about his ears and flattened it across his cheeks. His hooked nose and his arched brows now completely dominated his face. Simon looked at him and knew that, here indeed, was a real King of the Mountain.

And even as he thought that thought, the mountain trembled. Above them, all around them, the cave shook. The walls, the roof cracked. Earth fell like rain. And then, with a rumble and a crash, the stones from the walls of the farmer-kings came, like an avalanche, bursting from the tunnel, pouring around their feet.

Simon knew what had happened. Dewi had moved the Dancers of the Moon. In ignorance, he had used the power he had over the stone circle. The stones had moved. And, as the first Dancer had moved, it had fallen into the stairway which he had left open behind them. The walls, the stairs themselves, were wrecked. The way out on to the mountain was blocked. They were trapped.

13. Wizard Against King

The power in Dewi was terrifying. Simon could feel it. It seemed to radiate from him, dangerous, uncontrolled and violent. He feared that power

121

much more than he feared the thought of being trapped there in the moonlit cave.

Dewi looked dazed. He didn't seem to know what was happening. 'What was that?' he snarled at Simon. 'What was it?'

'It was you. You did it,' Simon told him, but he didn't hear him. Simon watched him as he stumbled around, prowling among the debris of stones on the floor. He coughed as he kicked at a heap of earth, and dust as dry as ashes rose in a cloud around him.

'Look at the mess,' he kept saying. 'Look at the mess.' And then, gradually, he seemed to begin to understand that they were trapped. 'Jones!' he said. 'Can we still get out?' He looked around, slowly at first, and then wildly. 'Jones, it's caved in—the stairs. It's caved in.'

'I know,' Simon said. 'I know. I—I think you'd better calm down.'

'Calm down! Calm down!' Dewi swore and scrambled and crawled over the pile of stones at the entrance to the tunnel and began to dig at it with his hands.

'It's no use doing that . . .' Simon began.

'No use?' Dewi turned and crouched there, glaring at him. 'No use? What to you mean—no use?' He began to climb, slowly, back across the rubble, advancing steadily across the cave, straight at Simon. His eyes glinted silver in the light from the walls. The Moon on his crown glinted like his eyes, and the diamonds shined hard and bright.

Simon gripped the Horn and stood quite still. He thought of the way he had used the Horn to fend off O'Shaughnessy's vine. If he had to, he would use it like that on Dewi. And, if that didn't work, well then, there was always the other way to hold it.

'How do you know it's no use? What makes you so sure?' Dewi's eyes glinted slyly. 'Did you plan this? Did you plan this with that—that death's head creature there?' Still he advanced towards Simon.

'No, of course I didn't plan this. And it's not what O'Shaughnessy planned either, I'm sure.' Simon tried to sound calm.

'But you *did* it, didn't you. You did *do* it. I think you're talking in riddles, Jones. I think you mean you didn't *plan* to do it, but you did *do* it so that you could trap me down here like Mamgu trapped him.'

'Mamgu didn't trap him,' said Simon. 'He escaped from Mamgu down here.'

Dewi didn't listen. 'You're against me, aren't you. You're like him. You're set against us Kings of the Mountain.' He was pointing at the skull now, and Simon didn't know who he was talking to. 'You hate us Kings.'

'No!' Simon said. 'You've got it all wrong. You've twisted everything I told you. And I didn't trap us here. *You* did.'

Dewi sneered at him unpleasantly. 'Being funny are we now, Jones,' he growled at him, and stepped towards him again.

'No!' Simon stepped back one step. 'Think!' he shouted at Dewi. 'Think! It all happened when you put the crown on.'

'You're lying!' Dewi shouted back at him. 'You're the same as everybody else. Everybody lies to me. I've had enough of lies—and I've had enough of that grinning idiot there too!' Suddenly he whirled to face the skull again. 'He's at the back of all these lies. It's him, that death's head. I'll get him for all this. So help me. I'll smash him, I will.'

He spun around, looking about him wildly, then leaping at the nearest, jagged rock, he tore it from the rubble and came back across the cave, lifting it murderously.

This was it. This was what Simon had been afraid of. Now he was going to have to fight Dewi. 'No!' He stepped in front of him, holding the Black Horn in both hands across his chest, like a barrier. Dewi stopped. He dropped the stone. Then he came on again. He reached out with both his hands and he caught hold of the Horn, wrenching at it. Simon held it tightly. That was all he had to do. The moment Dewi touched the Horn, the strength in it went through him in one great wave of power. It threw him back. His arms flew up above his head.

He reeled, stumbling helplessly, and then he fell, hard, among the rubble of stone wall. His face was twisted with rage and pain.

Simon advanced then. He was shaking. He hated this. He hated Dewi for making him do it. 'No!' he said again. 'No! No! No! You are not going to smash O'Shaughnessy. I won't let you. I'm not going to let you do anything like that. Never, ever! So shut up. *Shut up!*' Simon was almost screaming now. 'You did all this. You—you idiot!'

Dewi was still staring at him, but now he began to look confused. He said something in Welsh, shaking his head. Simon stood over him, still trembling. Then, gradually, he began to feel that Dewi was less dangerous, that the rage was leaving him, that he was growing calmer. Suddenly his head drooped, and he sagged limply, and covered his face with his hands. He was safe again.

Simon squatted beside him, then, with the Black Horn resting across his knees. He glanced sideways at the skull, and, for one wild moment, he had the idea that they were sitting there, Dewi the King of the Mountain, O'Shaughnessy the Irish wizard, and Jones of the Black Horn, all three of them, ready for a talk.

Dewi was looking at him again. 'Aw, Duw, I did do it all, didn't I. Aw, how did I do it? Jones, what happened?'

'It was when you put on the crown,' Simon said. 'I suppose you shouldn't have put it on yourself. You know, you should have waited until you were crowned properly, I think.'

'Jumped the gun, a bit, did I? Is that what you think?'

'Yes—I only *think* so. I don't know. But the way I understood it all was that you were going to have to be crowned, somehow, not just given the crown any old how.'

'No doubt you're right. Go on, say it. I'm an idiot. Say it. I know you want to,' Dewi said.

'I've said it already,' Simon told him, 'and, anyway, you couldn't help being an idiot, really, could you, if your mamgu . . . ' he stopped, not liking to say too much about Dewi's grandmother.

'Aw, go on, say it. It's the truth, ' Dewi said. 'Mamgu lied and lied and lied. Made sure Da never told me the truth neither, nor anybody else. It's Mamgu was the idiot. She should have known it was idiotic to interfere with things like this. She must have known it was an idiotic thing to do. But then, she didn't care.' He seemed to be almost talking to himself. 'She never cared two-pence about anything.'

'I'm awfully sorry she turned out to be like that,' Simon said.

'Well don't be!' Dewi sounded fierce again for a

126

moment. 'Don't sound apologetic about it, for pity's sake, Jones. There's no call for that at all. *I* don't care neither, not about her being like that, any road. Guessed it, hadn't I. Guessed it days ago. In Chapel, as a matter of fact, at the funeral. It was the phantoms, see. I never told you everything I thought about them. They were ghastly, Jones. Evil apparitions, I kept thinking. And then I thought so must *she* be, for they had come to take her off with them. And still I had to sing for them.' He looked away. 'It was a farce. It could have been so—so good. But it was a dreadful farce. There was Mam, in blissful ignorance. The Minister, aware that something dreadful was going on, but not able to see what it was. And Da, seeing it all but refusing to look. So I was the only one who watched—watched them taking her off rejoicing. And all the time I had to sing.' He turned back to Simon, and the silver light of the walls reflected from the moon on his forehead and flashed on O'Shaughnessy and on the Black Horn. 'No, I don't care about her being wicked. But she should never have taken my crown. That I can never forgive, so help me, never. Never forgive her for that Dark Army on my mountain, never, *never* forgive her for bringing the Kings of the Mountain to an end.' He bowed his head and took off the crown. 'For we *are* over. We *are*. I might have got my crown back, but one thing's certain, and that

127

is that I'll never be able to wear it. Not fit to wear it, I am . . . '

'Oh, for goodness sake, don't start feeling sorry for yourself.' Simon was amazed at himself. He wouldn't have dared say that to Dewi yesterday, but today, well, things had changed. 'It's because of the Black Horn,' he thought. 'It *is* better than the crown of the Kings of the Mountain, just like Fred said it would be—even though I didn't use it half as effectively as I could have done.'

'I don't like to hear you sounding sorry for yourself,' he said to Dewi. 'I don't like you much when you're being bigheaded, but I much prefer you like that to when you're like this.'

Dewi began to laugh. 'Duw, I asked for the truth from you, and now I'm getting it,' he said. 'Carry on. Jones bach, *I* like *you* like this.'

'I'm glad to hear it,' Simon said. 'Now perhaps we can work together like we're supposed to. Now perhaps we can work together and get out of here.'

'Wizard and King together, is it, then?' Dewi said.

'Yes,' Simon said. 'Wizard and King together.'

14. The Way from the Mountain

'Fred will have seen the Dancers move,' Simon said. 'I wonder if it's obvious from up there that the first Dancer has fallen into the stairway. I wonder if she can see that we're trapped.'

'By the look of all the mess down here, I should think it was more than obvious up there,' Dewi said. 'What a mess it all is.'

'If only I'd moved the Dancer back into place.' Simon said. 'I knew I should have, but I let you talk me out of it. If only I'd done it properly.'

'If only, if only! Fat lot of good it'll do us, you saying "If only",' Dewi said. 'Let's just concentrate on what to do to get out of the mess, eh.'

'All right.' Simon looked around at the smooth, silver walls. 'Well, I can tell you one thing now,' he said, 'and that is, if you're thinking of telling me to blast my way out, you can save your breath, because that is one thing I definitely do not intend to try.'

'Much to my amazement I find myself entirely in agreement with you.' Dewi looked at the walls too. 'No way do you interfere with that lot. Duw! Who made them, do you think? Who else was in on this Dancers of the Moon scene with us Kings?'

'Well, my book said something about elven folk giving you the crown,' Simon said.

'Who are they, for heaven's sake?'

'I don't know—unless—unless it's the people in the castle on the Islands.'

'That queen you nearly met?"

'Yes. Gosh! Do you know, I bet it was them. I bet they've got something to do with all of this. They're always watching, you know, watching the mountain and us on it.' Suddenly Simon felt very excited. 'Gosh! I've just thought of something. This, down here, the steps, this cave. It isn't just a *place*. It's a *way*. It's O'Shaughnessy's secret way to and from the mountain. It must be.'

'Jones, you idiot, you should have thought of that before. Duw, yes, the old beggar was on his way for the off with my crown . . . '

'Not necessarily.'

'No—OK, OK. He wasn't. Honest. I know he wasn't now, honest. But it must be his secret way back home, or wherever, so, like at the pictures, there's got to be an exit. Come on, Jones bach. Let's have a look around.'

Dewi scrambled across the rubble to the wall of the cave, and began to walk around it, looking at it carefully, feeling it, sometimes, with his hands. Simon wondered whether he should join him, but decided not to. He had a feeling that it would be far safer if he didn't touch the walls of that cave with his hands, and that he had better be careful about anything else he touched there, as well. He decided to put down the Black Horn, too, to make quite sure that he didn't use it accidentally.

The crown was still lying on the floor where Dewi had put it. Simon lay the Horn beside it. As he stood up, he looked down. The Black Horn, the crown of the Kings of the Mountain and O'Shaughnessy's skull lay in a triangle. 'A triangle . . . all three together.' He had thought that thought before.

Something, some impulse, some stray thought, made him step into the triangle. Instantly. O'Shaughnessy was beside him. There was no person there, no body. The skull still grinned from the same place on the floor. But O'Shaughnessy was there beside him. He knew it was O'Shaughnessy. No other presence would have felt so huge, rumbustious and strong. 'O'Shaughnessy?' he said. And then he heard O'Shaughnessy.

He heard him, quite clearly, as he had once heard the Unicorn, not with his ears, but inside his head. He didn't like it. It wasn't nice. The Unicorn had been wonderful. But this wasn't. A voice inside his head. No! He didn't like it. He didn't want to hear a voice. He didn't want to talk with anyone like this, not with anyone. But he could. And he had to. So he did. He stood quite still and stared at the skull.

Dewi noticed him. 'What's wrong?' Dewi had come quite close. He stepped away quickly. 'Why're you staring at . . . ? What's he up to?'

'He's telling me something,' Simon said.

Dewi swore and retreated still further.

'I have to—he's saying that I have to pick him up.' Simon felt as though his legs were about to buckle beneath him. He had to pick it up. That skull. That grinning skull sitting there, talking to him inside his head.

He did it quickly. Before he could think about it again, he did it. He stepped close. He picked it up. And, as he bent low over O'Shaughnessy he saw that he was resting on a trap-door. 'Here's why I had to pick him up,' he said. 'Here's the way out.'

'Aw, great!' Dewi ran across. He looked at the skull with distaste. 'Yeh, great,' he said to it, and he tapped it once with his finger tip. He looked at Simon and shook his head in disbelief and laughed nervously. Then he was brisk and enthusiastic. He pushed Simon aside. 'Move over, then, Jones. I'll soon shift this,' he said.

Simon didn't put O'Shaughnessy down again. For some reason—it could have been that O'Shaughnessy was telling him not to—he felt he mustn't put him down, so he stood there, with the skull held in the curve of his arm. He felt as though he and O'Shaughnessy were watching Dewi together, and, as they watched, Simon understood that O'Shaughnessy had planned that all this would happen. He had planned that, between them, they would manage to get trapped down there in that cave, and would then have to look for the other way out. Or perhaps it hadn't been a plan, exactly, but a gamble, and the gamble had been part of this plan, for he had to make sure that they didn't go back up on to the mountain, but took his other way out of the cave.

'Why?' Simon wondered. 'Where does it go, and why do we have to go there?' He felt as though he was asking O'Shaughnessy the questions, but O'Shaughnessy didn't tell him the answers. All he could do was stand there, and wait until Dewi had opened the trap-door. Then, perhaps, he would know why and where . . .

Dewi gripped the edge of the stone slab. He pulled from one side, then he moved around it and pulled and pushed from the other. 'Aw!' He couldn't move it. He began to swear. 'So much for us working together, Jones,' he said. 'It looks like I'm going to have to leave it all to you.'

'Only until you're crowned,' Simon said, and now he wasn't sure if he said the words himself or if O'Shaughnessy had said them. He must have sounded odd, for Dewi looked at him strangely. 'Half a tick,' he said, and that was him. 'I'll need both hands for this. I'll have to put him down. No, he doesn't want to be put down. You'll have to hold him.'

'Eh! Why doesn't he want to be put down?'

'I don't know. No—yes I do—it's to make sure that we don't leave him behind in here.'

'You mean we're going to take him with us!'

'Yes.'

'Jehosophat! How far? How long for? Are you going to be carrying him around for ever?'

'I don't know. I expect we'll find out. Come on— take him, please.'

Dewi grinned back at the skull as he took it, but he held it carefully, and stood aside with it, and now Simon felt that *they* were both watching *him* as he set his power against the force which held the thick, stone slab in place.

This stone didn't move easily. Simon needed all the power he could wring both from himself and from the Horn to move this one. But he did move it. And, as it slid away and uncovered the stairway which led from the mountain, a waft of fresh, scented breeze came flowing into the moonlit cave.

'It smells like azaleas,' Dewi said incredulously, 'azaleas and pine trees.'

'It's the smell of the Islands. This way leads to the Islands.' So that was where O'Shaughnessy's secret way led! Simon began to think and wonder.

Dewi was excited. 'That queen on the Islands . . . It's her behind all this. You're right, Jones. I bet you're right.'

'Let's hurry and find out,' Simon said.

'Yeh, right, OK. Great! Let's go!'

'Don't forget your crown,' Simon reminded him.

'Ah, yeh—all right. Better not leave it behind after all *he's* been through.' Dewi handed O'Shaughnessy back to Simon, and picked up the crown. He looked around, one last time, at the silver walls and the great, moonlit cave. 'I wonder if we'll see this again,' he said.

'Well, I wouldn't mind betting that *you* will, even if *I* don't,' Simon told him.

'Think so?'

'Yes, I think so. Now, come on, for goodness sake, let's get to the Islands.' Simon was beginning to feel excited. He was going to the Islands. For the second time in his life, he was going to the Islands, and this time he was actually going to step on to them. He suddenly thought of Fred. 'It's a pity Fred isn't here,' he said, 'but in a way it's just as well that she isn't.'

'She'd have been petrified,' Dewi said.

'Yes, but no more than we were—and I didn't mean that, anyway. What I meant was, Fred can't *see* the Islands so she thinks of them as not really there. So, would she have been able to walk on them, do you think?'

'Duw! And can we?' Dewi looked worried for a moment.

'Yes. Well, I did touch one before and it felt real. And O'Shaughnessy managed it all right.' Was he thinking this or was it O'Shaughnessy! It was strange, this mind-speak. He held the skull, not with distaste, but warily.

'Right!' Dewi said. 'Time we were off, I think.' He stepped through the dark, square hole in the floor of the cave on to the new stone stairway.

Simon followed him. As he stepped off the last step into the moonlit tunnel which led away seaward, through the mountain, he turned to look back to see if he could reach up to shut the trap-door safely. But the great slab of stone which he had found so difficult to move was already sliding itself back into place above him. Was that all part of O'Shaughnessy's plan, he wondered, or had someone else's plan begun to take over?

15. The Coronation of the King

Dewi sang softly as they walked to the Islands. He sang the song of the Kings of the Mountain, not the words, just the tune. He talked about it, too. He told Simon that he had learnt it from his grandfather. 'As soon as I could talk he taught me how to sing it, he said. Any road, I think that's when it must have been, on account of I feel I've known it for ever. Part of me it is. And it was Tadgu who made sure that's how it was. Made sure I could sing it by heart, he did. Made sure it was passed on, I suppose, no matter what Mamgu did—and Da . . . Not such an idiot as they say he was, was Tadgu, I reckon,' Dewi said, and, inside his head, Simon heard O'Shaughnessy agree.

The moonlit tunnel came to an end quite quickly. It opened in to a cave in a small cove at the foot of the cliff below the castle. It wasn't the cliff they could see from the carn. It was the cliff on the opposite side of that Island.

They stood still for a moment in the mouth of the cave, blinking in the sunlight, and looking out across this different, vast stretch of sea. On the horizon, mountains rose like dark clouds.

'That's Ireland,' Dewi said. 'I've seen that before, once or twice, from our carn, on a clear day. I don't suppose you can see it, can you, Jones.'

'Well, actually, I can,' Simon said. 'So it must be somewhere to do with magic.'

'Duw! I bet it's where our friend here came from. I bet he could see the Islands from over there,' Dewi said.

Simon waited to hear if O'Shaughnessy would mind-speak. He did, but not in words. All Simon felt was the deepest melancholy. 'Yes, he could see the

Islands from over there, and yes, that is his mountain we can see. Come on, let's not hang around looking at it,' he said quickly. He found the grief and homesickness in O'Shaughnessy too sad to bear. 'Come on, let's get this all over, for goodness sake.'

He turned his back on the sea and that distant mountain, and looked up at the castle. He had to lean back and crane his neck to look up at it, it rose so close and sheer above them.

'Is that her?' Dewi said suddenly. He was looking at the flight of steps which led from the castle down across the sparkling cliff to the quay which stood beside the beach. A woman in a gown which shimmered like dragon-flies' wings came so lightly down the steps that she seemed to float on the clear, sunlit air.

'Yes, that's the queen.' Simon smiled nervously. 'Look, she's beckoning. We'd better go over to her.'

'I'm for it now, I bet,' Dewi muttered.

'No, I don't think so,' Simon said, 'but let's not keep her waiting.'

They walked, quickly, towards the queen, and, as they came near her she bowed her head graciously, but not to them. It was O'Shaughnessy whom she honoured with her royal greeting. Simon thought that she wanted him to give her the skull. He held it out to her, but she shook her head, and he

138

understood that O'Shaughnessy was to stay with him, for a little longer, at least.

Then the queen looked at Dewi. She did smile at him, but not in the way that she had smiled at Simon and O'Shaughnessy. Somehow, her smile was both serious and stern as she acknowledged Dewi. And then she held out her hands for the crown.

For a moment, Simon worried. Surely she wasn't going to take the crown away from Dewi? Surely they hadn't done all this just to give the crown back to her? Surely she must know what a perfect King of the Mountain he would be? Surely she must understand that all he had to do was learn how to be King? He looked at Dewi. It was awful. That blank look was in his eyes again, that blank look which made him seem so terrible but so unhappy too. He was losing his crown. He *thought* he was.

But Dewi wasn't losing his crown. He was about to be given it, officially. Next moment it was obvious. This occasion, which Simon and O'Shaughnessy had made possible, and were now about to witness, was the coronation of the King of the Mountain.

When Dewi gave the crown to her, the queen turned with it in her hands, and held it high above her head, as though she was showing it to the castle triumphantly. Simon waited. There would be a

139

cheer . . . a jubilant cheer rising from the seven glorious towers.

But, instead of a cheer came stillness. And in that great stillness the queen turned slowly, and held out the crown to north, to west, to south and to east. Then, with a flourish, she held it towards the mountain. And the silver moon and the diamond stars flashed and shone and sent a beam of light across the shimmering sea towards the carn. And, back from the carn came one, clear, ringing note of music. It was as though the beam had echoed from the grey stones of the mountain top, for, although one was light and the other sound, the beam and the note had the same quality, they were made of the same substance. This, Simon knew, was great magic.

Then, as the ringing note faded and disappeared, the queen made Dewi kneel before her, and she placed the golden band, with its moon and stars, firmly upon his head.

The new King had been crowned. In spite of Mamgu, in spite of Amahiah, in spite of the Dark Army of the Cauldron, the Kings of the Mountain had not come to an end. Now, they could go on for ever.

16. The Return of the King

When Simon tried to remember it afterwards, he could never be sure at what precise moment the mood of Dewi's coronation changed. In fact, he wondered if perhaps it didn't change but was always serious and sombre in spite of the glory and wonder and magic of it all. It was certainly intensely serious when Dewi rose from his knees and the queen pointed to the mountain, and they knew that, now, they must go back together and fight against the Dark Army and win back the moorland kingdom for the moon.

At the far end of the quay lay a barge, flat-bottomed, with a sail like cobweb, silver with dew in early sunshine. The queen led them to it, and watched as they stepped down on to its deck.

As soon as they were safely aboard, the scented breeze filled the sail, and they began to drift away. The queen raised her hand gracefully to them. Simon saluted her with the Black Horn, and Dewi bowed his head, making the crescent moon flash its light across the shining cliff and up, up to the topmost pinnacle of the castle.

Steadily, they sailed past the other tall Island, where the pine trees grew, and there was the Unicorn, on the wide, white beach, watching, looking for Simon. It called to him, one pure, bell-like chime, and, oh, how he wished that the tunnel from the mountain had ended on that Island. But this was no time for the Unicorn. He could only salute it with the Black Horn, and watch as it reared and tossed its head, its mane floating like gossamer. 'I'll come back again. I will come back,' he called to it in his mind, and the Unicorn knelt and bowed to him, and he knew that it had heard and understood.

The wind strengthened, and they sped across the water. Beneath the rainbow they sailed, past the five, smaller, flatter Islands, and then, there was the mountain, so close, *their* mountain, all in darkness. It was night. There were no clouds. There should have been a moon but the moon still wasn't there.

'Look at it!' Dewi swore softly. 'Look at it, Jones. It's more dark than ever with my Dancer fallen. It's sort of empty . . . all the sky. Duw, there isn't even a star out tonight.'

Simon looked up at the sky above the mountain. He began to feel uneasy. What had happened? It all looked different. What else could have happened? 'I don't like the look of it,' he said.

Dewi groaned. 'Aw, do you think it's something I did, putting the crown on like that?'

'No, no. I—I don't think it's that. I think it's something else. It's something to do with the Dark Army.' Simon was listening for O'Shaughnessy, waiting for O'Shaughnessy to tell him what could be wrong. But all he could feel was a terrible foreboding about the army and about the Cauldron—especially about the Cauldron—and he wasn't sure if it was he or O'Shaughnessy who was so terribly worried. 'Probably me,' he thought. He didn't think of O'Shaughnessy as being a worrier.

He began to worry about Fred then. What had Fred done when she saw the Dancers move? She *must* have seen the first Dancer fall. What had she done then? Had she run to tell Daniel? And what would Daniel have decided to do about it? Simon looked up at that empty black space above the mountain, and worried even more.

As soon as the barge touched the beach, Dewi leapt ashore, splashing through the rippling waves. Simon waited until it slid up on to drier sand, then leapt after him. He turned, ready to watch the sail fill again, as the breeze changed direction and drove the barge back to the Islands.

But the breeze died away. The cobweb sails hung limp and empty. The barge lay still.

'What are you waiting for?' Dewi said impatiently.

'It—it ought to go back to the Islands. It can't stay here.'

Dewi came to stand beside him. 'Well, it isn't going to go back like that,' he said. 'Should we give it a push, do you think?'

'No—no. It ought to go on its own, with the breeze. It changes direction. *They* make it.'

'We-ell, if they haven't made it change direction, then they don't want it back yet, do they? Don't be an idiot, Jones.'

'Oh! I see what you mean! Of course!' Quickly, Simon worked it out. 'If the barge was meant to go back, then they would make it go back, and nothing would stop them. That means they don't want it back, yet. They want it to stay here. But why? It must be all part of their plan.'

'Yeh. Tell you what it reminds me of—Fishguard Ferry hanging about till everyone's on board ready to go.'

'Yes, that's it.'

'Who's it going to ferry back, then, do you think? Us?'

'I don't know. I just don't know. It'll be waiting until after . . . Come on! We'd better hurry. It mustn't still be waiting in the morning.'

They hurried across the sand and the wet stretch of marshy shore, to a lane which led up through the town to the mountain. As they walked they tried to plan what they should do. The Dancers had to be made complete again. That would be the first thing to do, and Dewi was the one who had to do that.

'What'll you be doing while I'm busy at that?' he asked Simon.

'I don't know. Keeping guard, I expect.' Simon listened to O'Shaughnessy. 'Yes, I have to guard you carefully while you move the Dancers and bring back the power of the moon to help us win the fight.'

'He's telling you all this, is he?' Dewi asked. Simon nodded. 'Well, for pity's sake ask him to give you a few tips on fighting and that, will you Jones, because I think you're going to need them,' he said. And, again, Simon felt that terrible foreboding—the Dark Army, the Cauldron. Something else had gone wrong . . .

They climbed, slowly, to the carn. They were tired. Even Dewi was tired. 'Jones,' he said. 'When we get to the top I'm going to call Caradoc.'

'Who's Caradoc?'

'The stallion, idiot. When I call him he'll come.'

'But you shut him in.'

'No problem! Caradoc'll get out of anywhere when he hears me call him.'

'How do you call him?'

'I whistle,' Dewi said, and that was what he did.

When they reached the carn, they stood looking at the Islands for a moment. Then Dewi turned towards the moorland and Castell Llewelyn, and said something, softly, in Welsh, which Simon thought must be a quiet thought sent to the pony.

Then he put his fingers in his mouth, and he whistled.

It was a piercing noise, a shriek, shrill and ear-splitting, a noise which could only belong and exist in the world of a King of the Mountain. It brought not only Caradoc to Dewi, but the whole herd of half-wild ponies. Across the moor they came, straight to their King, hooves thundering, manes tossing, tails streaming in the wind.

Dewi jumped down from the carn to meet them. He leapt from stone to stone, and then stood and waited in the middle of a level patch of low gorse and heather. Simon followed him, but stood higher up. This was a King's happening. This was dangerous.

The bodies of the horses rippled and gleamed with strength and vitality. Their eyes gleamed white as, wildly, they tossed their heads, and breathed breath like smoke from their flaring nostrils. The ground shook as they stamped and reared.

Dewi was surrounded. Simon saw his head, once, as the crown gleamed for one, brief moment. Then he was lost again, lost in the twisting, heaving mass of wild horses. Then Simon saw him on Caradoc's back, and jumped down from the carn as he beckoned.

'Take Non. She's quiet,' Dewi said, and held a dappled mare as Simon scrambled on to her back. 'You'd better let me take our friend.' Dewi held out his hand for O'Shaughnessy, and, gratefully, Simon passed the skull across to him.

Next moment, they were away, Dewi in front, with the crown on his head and the skull of O'Shaughnessy held high in his hand. Then Simon, with one hand tangled tightly in Non's mane, the other gripping the Black Horn. And the wild herd closed around them, hooves thundering, manes tossing, breath snorting from them in great gusts of steaming air.

It was exciting. Dewi was laughing. Simon shouted into the wind and heard his shout echo behind him. They would win. Who could stop them?

Who could touch them, Wizard and King? This was
their fight and they would win . . .

But, when they came near Castell Llewelyn, the
excitement faded, and a mood near to fear set in.
For it was not just one Dancer which had fallen.
They all had. The stone circle lay ruined, and behind
it the farm, the castle of the Kings of the Mountain,
stood in deep and terrible darkness.

17. Jones—Wizard and Warrior

Simon felt as though he was in the middle of a bad dream. He sat there, on Non's back, not really aware of where he was or what he was doing. All he could feel was a clear, cold emptiness. He could hear the emptiness. It vibrated. It screamed, one high note, as though someone, somewhere, had plucked at the taut, thin string of some ancient instrument. 'It's space—I'm lost in space,' was all he could think. Then he heard O'Shaughnessy inside his head; of course it wasn't space, he could breathe, couldn't he! 'What's happened?' he thought. He heard Dewi saying the words, 'What's happened?' He listened for O'Shaughnessy again. 'It's the Dark Army,' he told Dewi. 'They've left the moor and gone into the castle.' He saw Dewi look sharply at the farm, as he suddenly saw that it lay in darkness. 'They've invaded it,' Simon told him. 'It's something to do with the Cauldron. Someone in there interfered with the Cauldron . . . '

'Never Mam, never! Mamgu said *never*. What do we do now?' Dewi's face was bland and expressionless again 'Did the army wreck the Dancers, or did I?' he asked.

'You did—and you've got to put them right.'

'How can I?' Dewi's voice rang out like a cry of despair.

Simon almost gave up. Dewi mustn't despair. He mustn't start feeling sorry for himself. Not now! 'You can do it. You're King of the Mountain. Come on! Start the fight. Come on!'

Dewi was looking at the farm. He began to talk softly to himself in Welsh. He was worrying, grieving. It was harrowing to hear. Simon couldn't bear it. O'Shaughnessy was worrying too, inside his head, worrying, worrying, frantic about the Cauldron. And now, he too was beginning to worry, to feel frantic, about Fred. Where was Fred? Where was she? 'Dewi, please let's get on,' he begged. 'You've got to get in there among the stones. You've got to start to sing. I'll stand guard.'

'OK, OK, Jones—you and that Black Horn. Don't let me down, Jones, *please.*'

Simon knew what Dewi was really saying. He was really saying: 'Jones, *please* blast with that Horn.' He was *asking* him, *saying 'please'*.

'No, no, I won't let you down. I'll come in there. I'll stand there with you, and—and—I'll do what ever I have to do.' Simon couldn't say it either. He was too frightened. But he *would* have to use the Black Horn in all its power. He knew he would. If ever there was a time that the full power of the Horn was needed, that time was now.

They slid from the horses, and Dewi slapped Caradoc and shouted at him, and sent him careering off into the night taking the mares with him. Silently he handed Simon O'Shaughnessy, and then, together, they walked into the ruined circle.

Simon looked around. What a wreck! What a mess! Two of the stones leaned drunkenly, propped against each other. Another two had crashed back to back. One seemed to have begun to move towards the centre of the circle and then collapsed, face downwards. The rest had simply fallen and now lay at crazy angles—except for the first Dancer, and that had subsided into the open stairway and now stood there, half its usual height.

Dewi gripped Simon's arm just above the elbow. 'Stay with me, Jones,' he said. 'Stay with me, right beside me.'

'All right.' Simon had begun to shiver. 'I'll s-stay—right here.'

'Right, then. Right!' Dewi muttered to himself in Welsh. 'Right!' He clenched his fists down at his sides. And then he shouted. 'Right, you beggars!' He shouted at the farmhouse. Then he turned away from it, and he raised his fists to the emptiness above him and cried out to the moon. 'Lleuad!' he cried. 'Lleuad!' And then he sang.

The song of the Kings of the Mountain had been a protest in school, the song of a rebel, intended to shock and dismay. Here, among the Dancers of the Moon, in darkness and danger, it was a hymn of

151

defiance and of glory. Dewi sang, and his voice rose and filled the heavens. It touched the carn, it swept out to the sea, it carved, up, up through the emptiness and reached towards the stars. And the stones moved.

All around him Simon was conscious of shapes moving—of stirring and rumbling, of the crunching of crumbling earth and the crushing of dead sedge. But he couldn't watch. He was on guard. He had to watch the castle. And, as he watched, the Dark Army came.

Out from Castell Llewelyn it came, a grey horde, like a flood, thick and full of shapes, odd shapes, creatures, phantoms, ghosts of men-at-arms, all broken, mad and evil—and intent on victory.

It advanced. It rose. Like a wave it swept forward. It curved upwards, arched mightily, high, spreading, ready to crash, to engulf, to overcome the clear, pure sound of the song of this King who would win the mountain from them.

'King of the Mountain!' Simon screamed at it. 'King of the Mountain! King . . .' His voice came like a battle cry, and he swept the Black Horn up in an arc above his head, and leapt towards the phantom surge. He leapt, bringing lightning—blue and silver—crashing, thundering, echoing from the castle and the carn.

There came the shriek of a thousand long-dead voices. And then came moonlight.

And Simon and Dewi, Wizard and King together, stood in the circle of stones. The crown of the King of the Mountain shone like silver fire, and sparks of white light flew from the diamonds to mingle with the stars. And above the carn, the crescent moon shone down in beauty and serenity.

18. The Man Called O'Shaughnessy

'I've never seen anywhere so beautiful,' Fred said. 'This morning it was the bleakest, ugliest place in the whole world, and now it's the most beautiful, It's worth *everything* we went through, isn't it, Jonesy.'

Fred and Simon were sitting with Dewi in his room, looking out at the Dancers of the Moon standing in moonlight. Downstairs, Daniel sat in the kitchen with Mrs Llewelyn and Amahiah. They were all waiting for Simon's father to come and take them home.

Fred had told them what had happened to her, and what had gone wrong at Castell Llewelyn. She had run to Daniel when she saw the Dancers fall, and Daniel had organised a lift for them both in his nephew's car, and they had rushed off to Castell Llewelyn to try to persuade Amahiah to do something to help.

'But he wouldn't,' Fred said. 'He didn't even want to hear about it. Your mother got very upset,' she told Dewi, 'and she started going on a bit about your grandmother. You know, "She's the cause of it all," sort of thing, and, "Why do I have to have that dirty, old cauldron of hers still in my nice clean scullery?" And, of course, as soon as she mentioned the Cauldron, Daniel had to come out with everything *he* knew about it. And then your father—well, I've never seen anybody lose their temper quite like he did.'

'He raged,' Dewi told her. 'We all rage.'

Fred stared at him. 'Well, I wouldn't sound quite so proud of it if it was me who did it,' she said.

Simon saw Dewi glare at her, and quickly said: 'Go on. What happened next?'

'Well, he—he got into this blind rage.' She still insisted on saying exactly what she thought about it, in spite of Dewi glaring. 'And he rushed off to the scullery, shouting a great stream of Welsh of which I couldn't catch one single word, but it must have been about getting rid of the Cauldron, because that was what he tried to do. And then—oh lor, Jonesy, it was awful! The *things* all came charging outside. The moment he touched it. And we knew they

155

would all get in. And Amahiah had had a sort of seizure I think. And Daniel and your mother, Dewi, dragged him into the kitchen and up the stairs. And we all ended up in here. They wouldn't come in here, you see,' Fred told them. 'It was because of the Islands on the wall, Daniel said. The Islands saved us.'

They had talked about the Islands then, and Fred had been allowed to hold the crown for a moment. Then they talked about O'Shaughnessy.

'I couldn't believe my eyes, ' Fred said. 'One moment there were two of you standing in the circle and the awful things were rising up over you. Then there was that terrific flash you made, Jonesy. And when it cleared, there were *three* of you standing there.'

'Duw, yeh! Gave me a real fright, he did,' Dewi said. 'Turned round to say thanks to Jones here, and there, right next to me, instead of little Jones, was this great, hulking, hairy giant.'

'He wasn't a *giant*,' Simon said. He grinned. 'he was pretty big, though, wasn't he.'

'How did you do it, bach?' Dewi said. He was still very excited about it all.

'I—I don't know. I'd only just realised I must have lost him, the Skull, when I took hold of the Horn to—'

'To *blast* them,' Dewi said.

156

'Yes, well, and I was turning around to look for it on the ground, and there he was standing over me. I think it must have been both of us did that, you know,' he said to Dewi. 'I think it must have been the Black Horn within the circle of the Dancers of the Moon that did that. I don't think I could have done that on my own.'

'Oh Jonesy! You're not being modest are you? Brass bedknobs, I hope not.' Fred was back to normal again.

And now they were looking out at the moorland in moonlight, and Simon was thinking of O'Shaughnessy, the huge, bearded man, with grey hair half hidden by an old felt hat, shoulders like an ox, just as Daniel had said, and the long, strong arms of a wrestler. 'It's funny,' Simon said, 'he looked old but when he came in here and picked up the Cauldron and went off up over the mountain with it on his shoulder, well, he was walking like a young man, wasn't he?'

'Yeh! Singing like a young bloke, too,' Dewi said. 'Baritone—nice voice.' Dewi sang the song O'Shaughnessy had sung as he strode off:

'Fight and sing. Beat the drums.
See, Fianna's warrior comes.
Sing and fight. Who will dare?
O'Shaughnessy, the man of Eire'

157

'Now we know why that barge had to wait, eh Jones. Duw, I'm glad it was for him. Going back to the Islands, was he, do you think?'

'No, I think he was going back to *his* mountain. That's where he wanted to be. I think he said to me: "Let's get it all over" so that he could get back there. He'd been away an awful long time, hadn't he?'

'Who *was* he, Jonesy?' Fred said.

'I don't know, but I think I'll look him up in *The Historian,*' Simon said. And he did.

He couldn't find him when he simply thought 'O'Shaughnessy,' but when he imagined the man, and thought about him singing and carrying the Cauldron back to his mountain in Ireland, *The Historian* stopped at a page which looked rather like a diary. The first entry was about a man whom the writer called: '*He of ye Tribe Fianna unto whoSe immortal Spirritte be given ye Great Cauldron for Safekeepinge.*' There was no date beside this reference, or a name, but, on the next line of writing there was a date—759 Anno Domini, and a name—Oenghus— and it said that he was a '*man of great Stature who lievetthe upon mountains*'. The next line was about a monk called Padhraic who lived, again on a mountain, in 937 AD. After that came Ruadh O'Shea, who was a blacksmith in 1159. And after that came a journeyman pedlar called Tamat Lughaidh. He lived in 1303. '*Alle of theSe do verily be* one and the Same,' The Historian said. *'Alle do be ye Kepere of ye Cauldron.'*

Simon told Fred and Dewi about it, and they insisted that he must write another entry on that page. 'O'Shaughnessy, an Irish wrestler in 1920 and 1985.' Simon added beneath this: 'He also knew about space.' He had been thinking and thinking about O'Shaughnessy telling him 'You can breath, can't you!' when he imagined that he was in space. 'How,' he wondered, 'could he know about space at all? Nobody knew anything about that when he was alive before, did they?'

'You think he's some sort of time traveller, do you?' Fred asked.

'I don't know. I just don't know,' Simon said. 'I'm afraid it's going to be one of those things I'm going to wonder about for ever.'

Another thing which Simon wondered about was why the Dark Army was afraid of the painting of the Islands. He thought there could be something magic about the paintings, because Dewi, the King of the Mountain, had painted them.

Dewi painted in the Unicorn on his mural. Then he offered to paint the same mural on Simon's walls, and when Fred saw it she asked if he would paint it on her walls, too.

This all took several months, for Amahiah, when he heard that the walls of the stairway beneath the first Dancer had been ruined, decided that they must be repaired, and Dewi had to help him. But, when he wasn't building walls, Dewi painted, and, when the murals were all finished, Simon felt extraordinarily pleased about it. It seemed right, somehow that Castell Llewelyn, Tŷ Corn Du and Tŷ Corn Du Bach should be linked by the Islands.

He still can't understand why it should seem so right. But he thinks that, one day, something will happen to show him why. He's probably right.